LOVERS AND LONERS

STORIES

JEAN RYAN

MadeMark Publishing
New York City
www.MadeMarkPublishing.com
Cover design by MadeMark Media
Cover image Depositphotos

DEDICATION

To Mark McNease,
whose kind efforts and abiding faith
made all the difference.

CONTENTS

Chasing Zero

Garret has a head cold. Naturally he's in a foul mood. His world has stopped.

His supervisors won't be happy either. They need his nose, and especially now. There's a big contract looming and they want the formula he's been working on: an energy drink for a new company called Game On. Other flavorists could fill in, but when it comes to crafting power potions no one is better than Garret.

Energy drinks, Garret says, don't have to taste great, they just need something that suggests potency: spikey notes, a punishing edge. Carbonation is not enough. Garret is working with a chemical that makes your tongue tingle, along with another compound that turns your lips numb, at least for a minute or two.

He works for Perception, the biggest company in this city. They've been making flavors and fragrances forever, and on days the wind doesn't blow you can smell all sorts of things. Some days it's bubble gum, as if there's a big pink tent of the stuff stretched above our heads; other days, the odor of Peking Duck wafts through our doors and windows.

Most of our friends work at the plant (I say "our," but they're really Garret's friends). Every month or so Randy, Koby, Guy and Christie come over for pizza and beer. Randy is married, though I've never seen his wife. Koby and Guy are single—no mystery there. The oddest duck is Christie. Built like a wrestler, she's a one-of-the-guys kind of girl—swears like mad, loves to watch football, uses the word "dude." Her hair is platinum and she has a fake tan, but she's a long way from pretty. They always stay late, talking politics or sports or movies—anything but work. Firms that buy flavors from Perception do not want people knowing what deals they've made with the company, so everything is done on the QT. The smallest slip of the tongue and you're gone. Secrecy is such a big deal that outside the plant, co-workers don't mention their work, even to each other. Still, I've learned plenty. I've lived with Garret for over two years and he's told me some things you wouldn't believe, like why a certain company's French fries taste so good. I'm saving all these tidbits. I write them down in a little spiral notebook that I keep under the bathroom sink in a box of tampons. Lately, Garret hasn't been sharing any secrets and I bet he wishes he'd never confided in me. I want to think he stays with me out of love, but who knows?

I am at the kitchen counter quartering some nice fat Chandler strawberries. "Do you want some of these?" I ask.

He lowers the newspaper and looks at the bright heap of berries on the cutting board. "No thanks."

"Well, you have to eat something—you're sick. You want some toast?"

He frowns, considers. "Yeah, okay."

Garret is afraid of colds; he'd sooner suffer a broken arm. He starts thinking he'll never be able to smell again and I have to keep assuring him that he'll be fine.

The nose is everything, I've learned. We taste with our noses. We discover with our noses. We remember with our noses. The brain, Garret says, began with the nose.

My friend Dawna fell in love with a psychiatrist. He made good money and he was reasonably attractive, but she wound up leaving him because she couldn't shake the fear that he was analyzing her. I know what she went through. Living with Garret, I worry about how I smell, especially, you know, certain times of the month. As you can imagine, I'm extra careful, and not just with that. I get my teeth cleaned four times a year now.

I pop a slice of multi-grain into the toaster and pour a glass of orange juice, and then I use the tip of my knife to turn a strawberry into a little red fan, which I place on Garret's plate.

I look at food differently now; I think about the insides, the chemistry. There's a lot going on in this berry, hundreds of different molecules, some we can smell, some we can't—unless something is evaporating we can't smell it at all. In Garret's lab at the plant there are thousands of little brown bottles filled with different flavors. One time he brought one home for me that smelled just like a Mojito. He was proud of that one. I think they turned it into a breath mint.

It takes a lot of expensive equipment to break down the chemical structure of something and then figure out which molecules matter most. At Perception they call this process "chasing zero" and it can take years. Sometimes it feels like that's what I'm doing with Garret, trying to get to the truth of him. I listen to everything he says, even when he's just complaining, even when he's had too many Bud Lights; I watch how he eats his dinner, which foods he goes for first, what he leaves behind; I study the positions he sleeps in, the way he shoves a fist under his chin; I even open my eyes when we're having sex so I can see the expressions on his face. He grimaces a lot, makes faces that used to scare me. Sex is strange business.

*

After Garret leaves for work I feed the turtles. One strawberry apiece, plus a turnip leaf, a slice of mushroom and an earthworm. Richard always goes for the live food first; Liz goes for the most colorful—she loves berries.

Garret is not much interested in these turtles. He inherited Richard from a friend who died and I think he's still resentful of the care involved (even though I'm the one doing all the caring). Richard was a bachelor when I moved in. He spent his days moving back and forth between a shallow pan of water and the clay pot he hid under. The first time I saw him, alone in that big wooden box, I couldn't understand.

"You just have the one?" I asked, turning to Garret.

"He eats," Garret shrugged. "He's fine."

I did not believe that. I will never believe that. I read an article once about a man in California who wanted to stage a live nativity scene. He somehow acquired a camel for this purpose, which he decided to keep as a pet. This guy had plenty of land, the climate was suitable and there were no prohibitive zoning laws. Below the story was a photograph: this large improbable beast with a chain-link fence in front of him and vineyards in the distance. The new owner was standing a few feet away, pointing at the animal, a wide stupid grin on his face. And all I could think was how awful it would be to never again see your own kind, to be, as far as you knew, the last camel on earth.

Garret wasn't thrilled about getting another turtle, but when I told him I didn't mind being the one to clean up after them, he relented. An hour later I walked into The Lizard Lounge—the pet store where Garret buys Richard's crickets and cuttlebones—and there she was, a female Chinese box turtle posed on a branch in her tank, waiting for me. I brought my face close to the glass and she pulled her neck out of her shell and we got a good look at each other. She was even prettier than Richard. Her glossy shell was the color of dark honey and vivid yellow streaks ran down her neck from the back of each eye. The top of her head was brown, her cheeks were golden. Her expression was calm, resolute, infinitely patient, and my adoration was swift and fierce. I wanted to know what she knew.

Richard, I assumed, would be thrilled to have a mate, which is why I named her Liz. I wanted to see how quickly he'd come to her, so I set her down a couple feet away from him, stood back and waited. I am still waiting.

Two springs have passed and Richard, to my knowledge, has never approached Liz. When she noses up to him, he gradually turns his shelled back to her. And he does something else now that Garret swears he never did before: Every once in a while he stands up against the wall of his enclosure and hangs there for several minutes, as if asking, in his silent turtle way, for help. I don't like it when he does this and I tell myself that he is just stretching.

I wonder if he took an instant dislike to her, if Liz is simply not the mate he had in mind. I imagine myself as a pet: a great hand setting me in front of the only man there is. "Mate," says The Hand. What if that man disgusted me—worse, what if *I* disgusted *him*?

Time is what turtles have in abundance and maybe that's why they're slow to court. I still have hope for these two. I picture the day when I look into their box and find Richard on top of Liz. I can't speak for her, but it would mean a lot to me.

*

Washing the breakfast dishes, I manage not to drop or break one. I have a condition, something no one can seem to figure out. My hands will be fine and suddenly they won't be; they'll start to twitch and tremble, and I have to stop what I'm doing until they go still again. Sometimes the spells last only a minute or two; other times my hands shake all afternoon. It's not MS and it's not Parkinson's. One doctor said it could be an auto-immune disorder too new for a name. Garret says it's all in my head.

Naturally I had to quit my job. I made $64,000 a year as a dental hygienist, along with full medical coverage and free dental care. Now I have no insurance at all. If we were married, I could get on Garret's plan, but he hasn't made the offer.

When my hands first started to go wrong, he was concerned; he even went to a couple appointments with me. But after three months, six doctors and I don't know how many tests, he started getting annoyed. Now I don't dare talk about my hands; without insurance there's not much I can do about them anyway.

He wants to leave me, but I have this ailment and no income, and he feels trapped. That's what I think. He was getting bored with me even before this happened. He was all set to dump me, then this.

And the things he's told me, all those trade secrets he wasn't supposed to share. All it would take is one measly letter to the editor, a little human interest story about who buys what. You can bet he's thought about that.

*

Hell's Kitchen. That's what Dawna calls the company Garret works for. "No good comes out of that place," she said, which is something I told Garret one day, kiddingly, and he about went nuts. (He doesn't like her anyway. Dawna is overweight, and fat people irritate him. Garret himself is lean as a race dog.) I started to defend her, saying that some folks just like to go with all natural products.

"Does the cow know that there is no molecular difference between a synthesized extract and a natural one?"

I turned back to the laundry I was folding. I wished I'd never said anything.

"Does she have any idea what would happen to the vanilla bean crop if that's all we used? What a stupid bitch." Garret has told me about vanilla, how it's the world's favorite flavor, and thousands of tons of it are made from things like wood pulp waste and petrochemicals. You can even make it out of cow dung. Think about that next time you reach for a sugar cookie. Same thing with citrus— the key ingredient, citral, is found in all sorts of plants. The lemon sorbet in your freezer probably started out as a Chinese mountain pepper.

Never say "artificial" around Garret. He hates that word. He says that's where all the trouble started. "Crafted" is the term he and his buddies use. Another thing that makes him mad is when people assume that all they do at Perception is make bad food taste good. I came home one day with a package of white cheddar rice cakes and he poked a finger at it and said, "You know what these would taste like without the flavoring? They'd taste like baseboard." I don't blame him for being prideful. Along with creating the magic behind French fries and Easter candy, Perception makes good things taste better, which is pretty significant when you consider how hard it can be to get old people and cancer patients to gag down anything.

Dawna doesn't care that Garret doesn't like her—she feels the same way about him, which is why she only comes by when he's working. She thinks he doesn't treat me right. She says I have self-esteem issues from being a foster child and that's why I put up with him. I have my doubts about that. For one thing, my foster parents— I had three sets—were not terrible. In fact, after hearing what some kids suffer at the hands of their real parents, I'm glad I didn't come from one of those Leave It To Beaver homes. I lived in apartments here in Cincinnati, and yeah they were kind of crummy, but I had enough to eat and decent clothes, and I liked my last mother a lot. Her name was Bonnie. She was good at making the most of things. One day I came home and found her cutting up the newspaper. She was folding the pages into little fans and cutting notches to make snowflakes; the living room window was covered with them. She looked up at me and said, "You have to make your own fun in this world, Emily. It's nobody's fault but your own if you don't." I have a brother but I don't know where he is—I do feel sad about that. The other thing that's hard—especially when I'm filling out medical forms—is not having a clue about what diseases my parents had. (On the other hand, maybe it's better this way: If I knew what ailments I could get, I might start waiting for them.) I wonder sometimes if my mother's hands shook like mine, and if so, did anyone find out why.

I've told Dawna that Garret has a tender side she doesn't see. When his dog Ace had to be put down last year, Garret cried for three days; and he calls his mother every other week no matter what; and when I talk to him he listens, which is something most guys aren't good at. Garret isn't the best sex I've ever had, but we do pretty well—except for lately. I've been renting porn to spice things up and it helps a lot. Say what you want about porn films—they're demeaning to women (I think they're demeaning to both sexes), the actors have pimples, the acting is awful—all that's true, but a lot of people have jobs thanks to this industry and if it puts people back in the bedroom, well what's wrong with that?

I did tell Dawna that Garret's been acting more remote, not talking very much, and she shrugged. "Doesn't surprise me," she said.

"I'm worried that he might want to break up with me but he feels bad about me losing my job. And, you know, my hands." I looked up from the dishwasher I was unloading. "What do you think?"

Dawna leaned back in her chair and shook her head. "I don't think his conscience is that keen, sweetheart." She gestured at the dishwasher. "You cook his meals, you wash his clothes, you do the shopping—you even take care of his damn turtles. Why would he want you to leave?" I didn't say anything. I'm used to how blunt Dawna can be. "I wouldn't count on him marrying you though," she added.

I shoved the dishwasher door shut. "Who says I'm looking to get married? I'm not. Things are fine the way they are." This is a lie. I'd marry Garret in a heartbeat, and not just for his insurance. I love him beyond reason.

"Good." She folded her arms over her ample bosom and studied me with a small, knowing smile. Dawna is my best friend and nobody's fool.

*

In the summer Garret puts the turtle pen outside so that they can get some sun on their backs. Even though box turtles hibernate in the winter, it gets too cold here for the Chinese variety, so in the fall they have to come back inside and sit under basking lamps to make up for the sun. The lamps and other lights keep their enclosure at 75 degrees—any lower and they'd "brumate," which is like a false hibernation where they stop eating but keep using up fat and energy, meaning they could die. Keeping box turtles inside shortens their lives, but what can you do? It's not a perfect world for any of us.

Turtles are not near as rugged as they look. They get parasites and respiratory infections and funguses, and they dehydrate easily, which is why Richard and Liz spend so much time in their water pans. I have to wash out these pans every day and mist the pen with spring water, and every other week I switch out the bark. I don't mind any of this; I like giving the turtles a fresh start. They have to live their whole lives in a four-by-three-foot box and keeping it nice is a way of apologizing. In the fall I tuck in a few pine cones, also rocks and branches. These objects may not fool them, but deep inside their leathery bodies, where the healing happens, I think the turtles are soothed.

I am partial to Liz. I love her face. I know that turtles don't really smile, but the way Liz's beak is shaped, you'd swear that's what she's doing. I look at her and smile myself, and every so often I place my hand on her back and let it rest there. Liz is just under six inches long and her plated shell fits sweetly in my palm. Maybe some of what she knows is being transmitted into my skin. Maybe touch is a language we don't know the half of.

Richard is an inch longer and he never smiles. I guess he can't.

*

I finish the vacuuming, then sit down at the kitchen table and look over a community college catalog we got in the mail. I'm 36, still young enough to pick and choose. Garret told me one time that I should do something different with my life. "You're smart," he said. "You shouldn't have to clean teeth for a living." Garret never gave me much credit for being a dental hygienist, even though I made plenty of money and liked what I did.

"Doesn't it gross you out?" he said, not long after we met. "All those rotten mouths." He shuddered.

"They're not all rotten," I told him, "and no it doesn't gross me out."

Garret gave me a long look, his dark eyes pinning me —he's a handsome man, no one would argue that. He shook his head and frowned. "That's just weird."

I turn the pages slowly, overwhelmed by the range of careers, the fact that I can sit at this table and pick a life out of a catalog. Hazard one and I ruin the rest. I might as well put on a blindfold and choose with my finger. Only I can't. I have to think about jobs that don't ask too much of my hands.

Bakery Chef. Accountant. Teacher's Assistant. Hotel Manager. I like to cook but I suppose that's off the table. Accounting? Too much typing. Just as I start to imagine myself looking after children on a playground, my hands start to quiver. I hold them out in front of me and watch them move on their own. My heart pounds. It's happening more. This is the fourth time in the last three days. I shove my hands under my thighs and take deep breaths, try to think of something else.

It feels like I am lost and there is no one looking for me.

*

This summer Garret went on another "Flavor Hunt." Every three years Perception's key players get to go to places like Indonesia and South America, where they rifle the jungles for the next great taste sensation. I can understand Garret's participation in this; what I can't figure out is why they asked Christie to come along. Christie works with soy products, tries to make them taste like the burgers or sausages they're pretending to be. Last year she supposedly hit a homerun with "Wonder Dogs"—I tried them and, believe me, she's not there yet.

With scientists around the world ransacking what's left of our rain forests, searching for everything from treats to treatments, you might think there's not much left to work with. You'd be wrong. Garret says we have barely begun. Finding a new fruit isn't the hard part. Turning it into something you actually want to eat or drink, that's where the real work starts. Garret says that most exotic fruits taste awful. If they are not rejected right away, they are stripped down to zero and paired up with something we know and love— strawberries, peaches, bananas. Lots of exotics wind up nameless and are used to bolster other products. That's what happened with wild ginger—they figured out that it intensifies the pungency of spicy foods and cools off your tongue afterward.

I would love to go on one of these Flavor Hunts, travel over forest canopies in a hot air balloon, see how lemurs live. No way they'll let me, though. Garret won't even ask.

*

By the time Garret gets home my hands have stopped shaking

and the chicken pot pies I made from scratch are ready to come out of the oven. I pour him a beer and myself a glass of wine, and we sit down in the living room like we always do before dinner. He coughs a couple times and blows his priceless nose.

"How'd it go at work?" I ask.

"Fine."

"How do you feel? Can you taste that beer?"

"A little, yeah." He takes a long pull on his Bud Light and sets it down on the coaster. Garret is neat, which I appreciate. He never leaves wet towels on the bathroom floor or whiskers in the sink. Actually there's nothing out of place or extra in this sleek high-rise apartment. "He has no *soul*," Dawna murmured the first time she saw it. Without looking up at me he says, "I need to tell you something."

I can feel my heart speed up, my cheeks getting red. *This is it,* I tell myself, trying to prepare the part of me that will be hurt.

He lifts his gaze my way but can't hold it there. He looks back at the bottle he is spinning on the coaster and tells me, in a rush, that he is in love with someone else.

My spine stiffens; already, thank god, I'm beginning to hate him. "Do I know her?"

"Yes, you do." He looks up, almost defiant now. He aims, pauses, delivers. "It's Christie."

Christie? For one startling instant I see her: big thighs, gutter mouth; hair and tan just as fake as her hot dogs. I'm not exactly gorgeous but I'm a whole lot prettier than Christie. It takes me a moment to get my voice back.

"How long?"

"Since June."

My mind does a fast calculation. June. That was the month they were in Paraguay. Screwing in the jungle. Screwing here too, evidently—next week is Thanksgiving.

"I wanted to tell you…" he trails off, takes another swig of beer.

"I understand," I say. "You were chicken shit."

His eyes narrow at this and he stands up and heads for the kitchen. "You know we haven't been good for a long time," he says, his voice accusing.

"At least since June," I reply.

*

"Big surprise," Dawna said when I told her about Garret's confession. "Who is she, do you know?"

"Christie. His co-worker."

Dawna's mouth opened. "The one who comes over? The butch?"

I nodded. "That's the one."

Dawna frowned and looked out the window. "Guys will screw anything."

Loathing moved through me when she said this. All I could think about were those adult films I'd been renting the last couple months. The bastard had been getting Christie, me *and* porn.

We were sitting at the table in her kitchen, a large warm room that comforted me, the glossy apples and oranges heaped in a wicker basket, the loaves of bread on the countertop—raisin, sourdough, pumpernickel. There was bounty here; the kitchens I grew up in were nothing like this.

It took Dawna about half a second to invite me to move in with her.

I shook my head. "That is so nice, Dawna, but I can't let you do that."

"Oh? Where are you going to go then?"

"I don't want to be in the way."

"I have this whole house," she said, "and look at you—you're no bigger than a minute."

"I don't have a job," I said. "Not at the moment anyway."

"Yes, you do—if you want it. I need someone to help with the dogs. I could teach you." Dawna owns a mobile pet grooming service; considering the five employees she already has and this house she bought last year, she must be doing pretty well for herself.

"You don't like it, no big deal. You can do it till you find something else." She reached out then and touched my arm. "And don't worry about your hands. The dogs shake so much they won't even notice." She smiled at me. "You're going to get better, kiddo. You just need to get out of that apartment."

*

There's not much of mine at Garret's place and leaving doesn't take long. The only thing I need help with is the turtle pen, which Dawna helps me carry into the elevator, across the lobby and down the steps. Carefully we shove it into the dog grooming van. Richard and Liz are hiding in their flower pots. His back is facing out, but Liz is looking at me, her head tucked partway in her shell. She trusts me. I'm moving her life someplace else and she is willing to cooperate.

The turtles were all I wanted and Garret had no problem letting me have them. At first I was only going to take Liz. I didn't want her to live in the same box with a male who ignored her. I would get her a new box, a real mate. Then I thought: What if Richard is ready? What if two years is not so much time for a turtle to make his move? So I decided to give him another year. If he doesn't come forward in a year, I'll put another male in there and let him take over. Then I thought: Maybe that's what Richard needs, a contender. Maybe it's not his fault that the urge to reproduce hasn't kicked in—he just needs to fight for Liz.

Dawna doesn't give me a chance to get weepy. We are in and out of Garret's apartment in less than half an hour. I clear out my drawers in the bedroom, my clothes from the closet, the stuff I keep in the bathroom. The last thing I do is pull that little spiral notebook out of the tampon box and prop it against the mirror. Then I take a piece of note paper out of my purse and write: **Yes, I made a copy.** I draw a happy face and beneath that I write: **Best of luck! Emily.**

I didn't make a copy—turns out I'm not that sort of person. I couldn't resist writing the note, though. It's like Bonnie said, you have to make your own fun in this world.

In the Company of Crows

Susan rinsed a plate and looked out the window. In the darkness of the backyard, up-lights illuminated the sprawling trunks of the oak trees. The branches above could not be seen, but Susan knew they were filled with crows, each bird holding its chill place throughout the night. On winter days at dusk they came here to roost, circling and swooping and cawing until, one by one, they were all absorbed. Hard as you stared into the treetops, you could not find them.

No one could say for certain why they gathered this way. Some believed in the wagon train theory—safety in numbers. More than anything else, crows feared owls. Maybe they all made bets that the crow on the next branch would be the unlucky one.

It was true they were noisy and numerous, but Susan liked crows. She enjoyed their strutting authority. In the fall they dropped walnuts on the street for the cars to run over, a show that always gratified her. Often she would step in and assist them, would gather the nuts herself and crack them under her heel. You could not take a wide-angle view of nature, she learned; there was too much to be done, too much cause for despair. She could not save the rain forests, but she could give the crows a helping heel.

Philip brought the empty wine glasses into the kitchen. "Delicious dinner," he remarked. "You outdid yourself. I liked that lemon tart they brought, too. Did Miranda make it?"

Susan tucked a plate into the cupboard. "She did. It amazes me, all the things she still manages to do." Miranda had multiple sclerosis; soon the cane she used would be replaced by a walker. "Did you see her hands tremble at dinner?"

Philip nodded. "Even her speech is affected now." He walked back into the dining room and gathered the napkins. Pausing at the cupboard, Susan admired his impeccable posture, a legacy perhaps of his Arabic heritage. His bearing, his reserve, his intelligence, even his accent, evinced power. She could not imagine her husband using a cane, could not see him in any other way than capable.

"I wonder if a support group might help Ben, if he'd consider that." Philip was a psychiatrist. "I could give him some names."

Susan, who knew that Ben would not seek such help, kept silent. She and Ben had spent many hours talking about Miranda's plight, from the day of her diagnosis six years ago to just last week, when he had cried in her arms.

Sometimes it seemed she was getting to know him all over again, like tonight at the table when she was listening to one of his restaurant stories. Instead of studying his mouth, or his hands, or his forearms, she found herself looking at him whole, as she would any other entertaining guest. Lovers for nine years, they had turned, painlessly, into friends—or so it seemed; the territory was still fairly new. How this happened she had no idea. It was as if some force, knowing they could not manage it themselves, had stepped in and set them right. Because they could not live without each other, they had been allowed this benign arrangement; they could appear in society like everyone else and behave like the proper guests they were. Best of all, no one had been hurt. There was no other way to look at it: They had won.

*

Susan had met Ben in her store, Big Dog Bakery. He and his border collie had walked across the threshold, then stopped short, obviously unprepared for the bountiful assortment, all the outrageous replicas of human food: oatmeal donuts, cheesy éclairs, carob-filled cookies, mini garlic pizzas. "Can I help you?" Susan asked. Ben approached her. His close-cropped hair was white, though he didn't look much over 40, and his skin was ruddy. His eyes, a nearly transparent blue, made her think of a jungle cat. A small scar hooked down one cheek. "This is *dog* food?" he asked.

She nodded. "But you can eat it, too—if your dog doesn't mind." He smiled at her. They held each other's gaze for a second, maybe two, appraising one another with pleasant surprise, and later Susan wondered if this was the point at which she hurtled into love, if attraction could be that swift and compulsory. Not that she was trying to excuse herself—there had been time enough in nine years to make corrections.

Could you even call it an affair? Wasn't there a more apt term for such a durable liaison? Naturally they had tried to extricate themselves, had retreated and returned more times than she could count. Eventually they gave up and, in tacit agreement, made room for their obstinate romance until it finally slipped away on its own. Now they were exonerated. Legitimized. It did not feel like luck. It felt like forgiveness.

*

Crows play—many people didn't know this. Susan had seen them engage in all sorts of recreation. Aerial loops, rolls and dives; sometimes they hung upside down from branches, played tug of war with twigs. Susan had seen a crow amuse himself with a discarded pack of cigarettes, dropping the object from a high branch and catching it before it hit the ground. Once she had started her own game with the birds, tossed a ping-pong ball near the trees and waited to see what would happen. Sure enough, one of crows flew down to inspect the ball, then snatched it up and carried it to the top of a tree. A moment later he let it fall, then swooped down and retrieved it. Seven times he did this.

Philip did not play with the crows. He was bothered by their noise and only wished they'd roost in some other Piedmont backyard. As if knowing this, the crows scolded him when he was raking leaves or trimming the laurel hedge; if he ventured close to the oak trees they grew even more boisterous. Susan could walk anywhere she pleased and the crows simply watched her.

One of oddest things they did—Susan had seen this only twice—was sprawl on the ground. On both occasions, the night had been especially cold and the morning sunny. She had been making toast the first time she saw them: twenty at least, all motionless, most of them twisted oddly, their wings pressed to the earth. Fear clamped her chest and she hurried outside. Not until she got quite close did they rise, all at once, and fly into the trees. They must have been warming themselves, Susan figured, and the second time it happened she did not disturb them.

*

In a world of staggering need, Susan acknowledged the frivolity of a bakery for dogs, but she adored her shop, with its wholesome odors and pure intentions. All the baked goods were natural, made fresh daily, and, despite their sinful appearance, most were low-calorie. But people came to her store for more than the treats and toys. They came for respite, for reassurance, and Susan delighted in spending her days among them, these people who could not do enough for their pets. Every purchase was a surge of devotion—surely the world had need of that. And then there were the lost and found notices she posted, the adoption photos, the ASPCA donation box next to the register—all these things mattered.

Philip had financed the shop, and while he knew his wife was no fool, the money she'd made, in just four years, surprised him. They had even begun to talk about opening another store in San Francisco. Ben, who also owned a successful business in Oakland's Rockridge district, a "fast food" pasta shop, was all for the idea. Once, flushed with wine, he and Susan had excitedly discussed the possibility of a partnership, and then fell silent, seeing how wanton this notion was.

Something they had not discussed—not seriously, and not for many years—was divorce. Miranda and Philip were fixtures, bearing walls, a fact that became clearer as time went on. In the beginning, there were moments when Ben would make some passing reference to Miranda, and Susan would harden with jealousy. Later this jealousy went away, replaced by wan affection, eventually pity: Susan had embezzled from this woman, steadily and with cunning; she could not hate her too. Only with deference and vestiges of shame did Susan and Ben speak of their spouses now. In fact, Susan wished Miranda could hear some of the tender things Ben said about her.

Susan had seen some pictures of Miranda "in her day," when her red hair was long and her clients were many, when she could still mount the steps of their fine homes. An interior designer, Miranda had done a flawless job with her own home, and walking through it that first time with Ben, Susan had studied the unlikely wall colors, the mix of exotic furnishings, envying this flair she would never possess.

They were not alike in any noticeable way. Miranda was short and slight and impeccably groomed. She wore scarves and gorgeous boots. She was quiet but not irritatingly so. (Ben said she could get "snappy," though Susan had never witnessed this.) Her features were finely drawn, giving her an inquisitive look. She reminded Susan of a small red fox. Miranda was 50 and wore it well, especially given her illness.

Blonde and big-boned, Susan did not know what sort of animal she might be likened to—a Guernsey cow maybe. She was also five foot ten. Ben once called her "majestic," a term that made her laugh but pleased her too. It helped that she was attractive. To be ample and ugly—she could not conceive the effort that would take.

*

Susan had read that crows mate for life, that only if a crow perishes will its partner seek a replacement. In the springtime she watched their courtships: the female holding close to the ground, the male circling her, his wings wide and drooping, his head bowing, his cry an insistent rattle. The crows all looked the same to her, large and glossy—who knew how they chose each other, what standards they used, and if the rejected suitors felt disappointment.

Watching from the patio, Susan often saw these pairs grooming one another. She didn't know who was doing the cleaning, the male or the female, but one bird approached submissively, head feathers raised, and the other did the cleaning, mainly the neck and face, those hard-to-reach places. With their formidable beaks, it's a wonder the crows didn't hurt each another. Maybe they did—birds could make mistakes. She had once seen a hawk miscalculate. Aiming perhaps for a mouse, it met the front end of a semi. A witness to this abrupt, bizarre death, Susan had to pull over and collect herself. There was a wrongness to it, a creature this magnificent felled by blunder. It shook your faith, made you afraid for everyone.

*

Not once had Ben spoken of his sex life with Miranda, and Susan had been equally discrete about her relations with Philip. This area was inviolate, a layer of betrayal to which they would not descend, and maybe it was this small tether to decency that had salvaged them in the end.

Susan did not miss the physical relationship she'd had with Ben, which struck her as odd. There were times—*there were years*—when all she wanted to do was be with him or think about him, when she spent blissful hours evoking their most recent tryst, replaying each reel in thrilling detail.

She had not known this overriding passion with Philip—not that Ben had special talents or that Philip lacked ardor. They were different, that was all, and they struck different chords in her. One evening she and Philip were watching television and an ad for Viagra came on. Idly curious, Susan asked him what he thought of it. "Ridiculous," he said, and she had smiled at him, involuntarily, out of sheer admiration. From what she had read and heard, this view was not common. Soon after, when she posed the same question to Ben, his answer was likewise brief but quite different. "Why not?" he said with a broad grin. Ben was 57. At this point perhaps he had more than a passing interest in the remedy. She had no way of knowing—they had not been intimate in many months. In any case, she was glad that Philip eschewed the drug. Things were fine the way they were, thank you very much.

Viagra. Talk about false advertising. Women had been faking orgasms, with unarguable success, since time began. Now, with blue diamond-shaped pills, men could perform their own magic tricks, and they were going batshit crazy. Unlike women, they were not much concerned with secrecy: Cozy TV ads for Viagra aired during the dinner hour. Men slayed her. In the same way that they happily accepted big fake breasts, they prided themselves on their own bogus erections. Women would not allow themselves to be scammed that way. A woman with silicone breasts never forgot what she was working with.

*

After courtship, the crows built their nests in the oak trees, big roomy baskets high up and close to the trunk; it took them a week or two. Each spring Susan watched the process from the patio. Both partners took part, soaring off and coming back with twigs, moss, bits of cloth, and afterward the females enjoyed a nice vacation. Before, during and after egg-laying, they sat on these comfy nests while their steadfast mates took care of them, returning again and again with all sorts of treats—crows seemed to eat anything, Susan had noted, from limp French fries to squirming insects.

A few times Susan had seen a lone bird cruise to the nest as soon as the spouse took off. She had researched this and learned that sometimes an unmated crow will take advantage of the sedentary female while her spouse is out looking for food. Presumably less robust than a chosen male, the unmated crow confers no genetic advantages, and so these couplings are considered pointless aberrations. What the female thinks of them is her own business.

*

Susan wiped the counter clean and shut off the lights in the kitchen. She paused in the room and looked once more at the oak trees.

She thought about Ben and Miranda, wondered what sort of rituals attended their bedtime: if Ben helped her undress, if they still made love, what they were like alone together. She was glad for them, she honestly was.

And then she had another thought, there in the dark, a thought that widened her eyes. She was still in love with him. She had not lost interest—her body had.

All this time she'd been preening, congratulating herself on achieving the impossible. That she and Ben were behaving like friends, this was no achievement, no proof they'd been forgiven. A light blanket of amity had been pulled over them to ease the chill. That was all. They had not turned good. They had turned old.

Susan looked at the trees and thought again of the crows crouched along the limbs. They slept standing up, she'd read, their heads resting on a shoulder, their eyes closed. Harm could come from anywhere.

She wanted to see them. She couldn't wait for morning.

Manatee Gardens

They were sitting in the too-warm kitchen, drinking instant coffee. Peggy looked past her mother's head and through the window. Snow was falling in the backyard, covering tree limbs, mounding in the stone bird bath. At the top of the window hung a plastic Santa with a sack slung over his shoulder and the words 'Merry Christmas' beneath his boots. This was a reliable decoration, appearing each year at this time, and much of the paint had flecked off. Peggy turned her gaze back to the lazy Susan and with one finger slowly spun it round. She had done this as a child, watched these same items revolve: a jar of instant coffee, a white sugar bowl, a pair of ribbed salt and pepper shakers. From the rug beside the back door, Frankie, the aging fox terrier Jan had rescued from the pound, yawned audibly.

"What do you want for Christmas?" Peggy asked.

"I want to swim with the manatees," Jan said.

Peggy stopped the lazy Susan and gaped at her mother. "Since when?"

"I love manatees," Jan said fiercely. Her blue eyes flashed. As if in defiance of her 78 years, her eyes were bright and still beautiful. As always, her hair was pulled off her face and tied in a ponytail; she had been a natural blonde and the transition to silver had been subtle.

Peggy frowned. It was just like her mother to say this sort of thing, to come up with some sudden, peculiar whim, probably fueled by a program she'd seen.

"You get on a boat and go to them," Jan went on. "You wear a wetsuit."

"Where's this?"

"Florida. I have a brochure." Jan rose stiffly and opened a drawer behind her. As usual, she was wearing black stirrup pants and

20

one of the aggressively cheerful sweatshirts she bought at the mall. Peggy noted how small her mother's back looked now, how thin her calves had become. It was true: she was shrinking.

"Manatee Gardens, it's called." She pulled a flyer out of the drawer and slid it across the table. Peggy glanced at the photos: a catamaran, a grinning captain, turquoise water studded with fat brown humps.

"They're closed on Christmas day but not on Christmas eve," Jan said. "That's when I want to go."

Peggy looked up from the brochure. "Are you kidding? It'll be a zoo!"

Jan shook her head. "It's not a zoo. It's their home."

*

Merging onto the Pike, Peggy thought, *why manatees?* If her mother wanted to swim with dolphins or turtles, like everybody else, they'd be headed to the Bahamas or Maui, not some Florida tourist trap. She could see the place now: a worn-out gift shop with key chain bobbles and dusty jiggers, a few torpid reptiles in smudged terrariums, a leather-skinned, bleary-eyed skipper handing out life vests to shrieking children.

At least her mother had given up the notion of holiday travel and agreed to a mid-January trip. And it wasn't like they'd be gone very long—a three-day weekend would probably suffice. And even if they weren't heading for some swank Caribbean resort, at least they'd be getting a respite from the brown snowbanks and ice-crusted sidewalks of the eastern Massachusetts. They would make the most of this trip, Peggy decided, changing lanes, and her lips tightened in accordance.

She would take care of the travel plans, she told her mother, and Jan had shrugged. "Okay," she said. "But no frills." What Peggy really wanted to do was get a peek at her mother's checkbook. Not long ago, Jan had written a generous check to a crook who appeared at her door asking for donations for children in need of facial surgery. "He was wearing a suit," she explained.

It wasn't just her mother's trusting nature that concerned Peggy; it was her recent difficulty with words. Today she'd been fine, but when they met for lunch a month ago, Jan had opened her mouth to order a sandwich and had not been able to speak. "I want," she began, and then her eyes widened and she looked at Peggy for help. Peggy blinked at her. "What do you want, Mom?" Jan said nothing, just shook her head. Peggy reached across the table and laid a hand on her mother's arm. "Just point to it," she said, and Jan did as she was told, tapped the picture of the grilled cheese sandwich and nodded at the waiter. Peggy ordered her own sandwich, and when the waiter left she turned back to her mother. She was going to tell her it was fine, that everyone forgets their words now and then, when Jan smiled at her and said, "Well wasn't that the damndest thing."

"The brain is circuitry," her husband explained that night. Philip was a vascular surgeon at Brigham and Women's Hospital. "With age, disease, the wiring fails." Peggy pictured this, wires sparking and shorting, regions going dark. And her mother was aware of this, knew that her mind had turned treacherous. Peggy could not think of anything more dreadful, and she was baffled by her mother's calm— at least she *seemed* calm.

A check-up and cognitive tests revealed nothing, nothing tragic at any rate—manageable degrees of osteoporosis and arthritis, slightly elevated blood pressure; all her labs were normal. As for Jan's language difficulties, there were drugs they could try if the condition worsened. "But we'll sit tight for now," the doctor said, rising from his chair. Jan turned to Peggy. "I told you I was fine. Now let's get out of here."

*

Snow and heavy traffic hampered the trip home, and it took Peggy nearly an hour to drive from Shrewsbury to Newton, a commute she made every couple weeks. One day her mother would probably be living with them, which would solve the travel concerns, but Peggy could not yet allow herself to contemplate this arrangement; each time the thought crept up, she pushed it back down. Philip was actually fine with the notion of Jan moving in, maybe because he had lost his own parents many years before, or maybe because he simply and truly liked Jan. He said she was "a kick." Jan *was* a kick, Peggy agreed, but this had no bearing on what her daily presence here would do. Peggy loved her husband for his generosity, but really, he had no idea.

She walked into her house and switched on the hall sconces. At some point in the afternoon, witnessed by no one, the roses on the granite table had fallen from their stems, and the white petals on the black surface looked like art. She stood there a moment, admiring this small gift, before hanging up her coat and heading into the sleek kitchen with its cherry cabinets and stainless steel appliances. This was an older Craftsman home, but renovations over the past five years had turned each room new and close to flawless.

Philip had surgeries today and would not be home till at least 7 pm. Peggy poured herself a glass of Pinot Gris and fixed a small plate of goat cheese and crackers, which she carried into the study and set beside the computer. She needed to make flight reservations right away and to see what sort of accommodations she could secure at this late date. Jan did not want Peggy paying for this trip, but Peggy was firm, reminding her that this was a Christmas present, and it was. It was also insurance. They didn't have to stay at the Grand Hyatt, but Peggy would not have them wind up in one of those budget monstrosities, besieged each spring by crazed college students.

*

For the flight to Tampa, Jan brought a box of art markers and a book of circular designs, which she steadily filled in with color. Peggy, who had never seen a coloring book intended for adults, asked her mother where she found it.

"Amazon," said Jan. "It's called 'active meditation.'" She slid a teal marker out of the pack. "These are mandalas—sacred circles. They're supposed to be calming."

Peggy smiled. "Are you calm yet?"

Jan shrugged. "I just like coloring them in. It's something to do." She looked up at Peggy. "You want one?"

"No thanks. I have my book." But the writing was god-awful— Dan Brown should have stopped after The Da Vinci Code. She kept looking up from the page and out the window, where crumpled mountain ranges and patchwork farmland slowly slid beneath them; to the left was the shimmering Atlantic. She checked her watch: one more hour.

"I think I'll take one of those pictures, Mom."

Jan set down her marker and carefully pulled a page—they were perforated—from the back of the book. She handed it Peggy, then bent back over her work. "Start on the outside," she advised. Peggy pulled an orange marker out of the pack and began coloring in the border of an intricate circle. "My god," she breathed. "I see angels." Her mother ignored this, and after a few minutes, Peggy found herself absorbed in her picture, giving thought to the shades she chose and leaning back to see the effect. When she heard the pilot announcing their descent, she was surprised.

Jan pushed up her tray table and tucked the mandala book back in her bag. She looked about the plane with pleasant interest, then leaned back and closed her eyes. Peggy regarded her profile wistfully, thinking how pretty her mother was, how good her neck and chin still looked. Peggy would not be that lucky, did not have that sort of bone structure. She was 55 and doubted anyone would guess her any younger. From her father she had inherited her square jaw, as well as her tallness, and now that her estrogen was gone, she had his waistline, too.

"Is Carolyn taking care of Frankie?" Peggy asked. Carolyn was Jan's next door neighbor and oldest friend. She too had lost her husband several years before.

Jan opened her eyes and turned to Peggy. "She's staying in the house, bless her heart."

"That's sweet of her. Frankie will like that."

Peggy looked out the window again. Tampa looked infinite. Toy cars moved along toy highways; here and there were the turquoise lozenges of swimming pools. The drive to Crystal River, she'd read, took about an hour and fifteen minutes; she'd have to remember to ask for a car with navigation.

"So mom," she said, turning back to Jan. "What is it about manatees? Why the big urge to see them?"

Her mother didn't speak for so long that Peggy thought she had once again lost the ability. Jan had never been a talker, which was frustrating at times, but better, Peggy supposed, than a mother who never shut up.

"You know they call them sea cows?" Jan said at last. "They're *huge*. They don't harm anything. They just swim around eating plants."

"Are you sure you'll get to see any?"

Jan nodded. "This place we're going, Kings Bay? The manatees go there every winter—they can't take cold water. It stops their digestion."

"I suppose they're endangered," said Peggy.

"Oh yes." Jan sighed. "Boats hit them."

Peggy waited for something more intriguing, but her mother had closed her eyes again and had nothing else to say.

*

It was late afternoon when they finally pulled into the hotel. Peggy's eyes were tired and she had a ferocious headache. Despite the car's navigation, they had taken the wrong exit twice and traffic had been terrible.

"I need a drink," Peggy said, stepping out of the car. "Pronto."

Despite the thick cloud cover and cool temperature—66°F according to the rental car—she could feel the humidity close in around her. Across the parking lot, the hotel rose before them like a promise kept, just as attractive as its online photo.

"Sounds good," said Jan, who, with some effort, emerged from the car and looked around. She gestured at the hotel. "It's….."

Peggy waited a few seconds, then finished the sentence. "It's new. It's supposed to be nice. I'll check us in and be right back."

Their rooms were adjacent and located on the top floor, removed from footfalls and ice machine noise. Pushing open the reassuringly heavy door, Peggy paused to take in the amenities, gratified by the room's soothing colors, the immaculate King-size bed (wisely minus a spread), the faux mahogany furnishings. No matter how the rest of the weekend went, at least they had these separate, pleasing rooms in which to repair. Jan of course did not approve of this arrangement, had already protested the extravagance of two rooms. Peggy, knowing her mother would react this way, paid her no heed.

Frugality, Peggy had learned, was a habit, one she'd eventually broken free of. Thrift could get the better of you, could close a lot of doors. Her father had been frugal. For 32 years he owned a shoe store in downtown Shrewsbury, never changing out the old carousel racks or revamping the front windows, paying no attention to the more fashionable businesses that shouldered their way in. As a child, Peggy had loved her father's store, loved trying on all the new shoes and admiring them in the little floor mirrors, but as she got older these feelings changed, and the store became an embarrassment. For one thing, it was called Sheldon's Shoes, which would have been fine except that Sheldon was her father's first name. Sheldon's Shoes sounded like one of those elaborately illustrated children's books, a pair of penny loafers on the cover, all ready for their big day. The fact that nothing in the store changed, that year after year people sat on the same olive green Naugahyde seats and turned the same creaking displays depressed Peggy beyond speech, and when her father finally sold it, two years before he died, she was glad to lose the association. Predictably, her father's income had been modest, but if he had not been a canny businessman, he had been shrewd in other areas, surprising his widow with some well-timed investments and a life insurance policy that more than covered her monthly bills.

The desk clerk told them about a nice restaurant not far from the hotel, and so Peggy and Jan decided to walk there. A strong breeze blew against them as they made their way down the wide asphalt path that bordered the highway. How strange this place was, Peggy thought, this flat, open land with its random businesses stretched along the road, a pawn shop here, a hair salon there. Trees grew in disparate clumps, bare, twisting limbs entangled with ivy-choked pines. Lanky palm trees swayed in the wind, their fronds waving and snapping. Just as Peggy and Jan reached the restaurant, rain drops pattered their heads and shoulders.

"Hope it's not pouring when we leave," said Peggy, smoothing her hair. "Do they still give tours when it's raining?"

"I don't know why they wouldn't," Jan said.

The restaurant was dimly lit and nearly empty; it smelled of fried fish, varnished wood and a potent disinfectant. A smiling, chunky hostess led them to a booth and handed them large leather-bound menus. "Enjoy your evening," she said.

Peggy pulled her reading glasses out of her purse and opened the menu; Jan, who'd had refractive surgery, did not require glasses. "God almighty, look how small the print is—why do they *do* that?" She scanned the list, frowning. "Wow. They really nail the tourists here—$29 for a pork chop."

Jan closed her menu and said, "I'll have a Manhattan and the Vintage Seafood Platter."

Peggy set her menu on top of the other and removed her glasses. "Guess I'll have the grilled grouper."

A server appeared at their table, a black woman with thin glossy braids that fell over one shoulder. Tidy, perfect rows crisscrossed her scalp. "Can I get you ladies something from the bar?" she said. She had a Cajun drawl: half deep south, half Caribbean.

"You sure can," said Peggy. "I'll have a Stoli over and she'll have a Manhattan."

"Be right back," said the woman, picking up the menus. Jan watched her walk away.

"I like her hair."

"Must take forever to do that," Peggy said.

"They call them cornrows," said Jan. "Black people spend a lot of money on their hair."

Peggy smiled. "How to you know that?"

"I saw a show. They buy hair and make 'weaves' out of it. Do you know where the hair comes from?"

Peggy shook her head.

"India. Indian women are afraid to go to sleep because people cut off their hair when they're sleeping." Jan nodded. "It's true."

Peggy, absorbing this, said, "Mom, you are one surprise after another."

Both their meals came with a salad: iceberg lettuce on ice cold plates with a few pallid wedges of tomatoes and some shredded carrot. Peggy got through about half her salad, then watched Jan chase the last bits of carrot on her plate. For a small woman, her mother had an astonishing appetite.

"When do we have to be at Manatee Gardens?" Peggy asked.

"6 am."

"In the morning?"

"The boat leaves at 6:15," Jan said. "But we need to be there early to see a video. And we have to put our wetsuits on." She pushed her empty salad plate to the side.

"*I'm* not going swimming. People can just stay on the boat, right?"

Jan blinked at her daughter. "You're not going in the water?"

"Do you know how cold that water is?"

"72°."

Peggy nodded. "That's pretty damn cold."

"That's why you wear a wetsuit."

"Yeah, I know." Peggy leaned back against the booth and folded her arms across her chest. "But I'm just not that interested. This is *your* deal."

Jan shrugged. "Suit yourself."

The mustard sauce on the grouper was a little too spicy for Peggy, but she managed to eat around it. Jan proclaimed her own meal "scrumptious," and Peggy watched, faintly envious, as her mother made steady progress through the fried shrimp, scallops and onion rings, just the sort of food she herself couldn't tolerate, not anymore; she wouldn't sleep a wink.

As Peggy and Jan were leaving the restaurant, a family came streaming in: an exhausted-looking couple with three children and an infant. The baby was crying.

"Glad we missed that," Peggy said. She pushed the door open for her mother and they stepped into the cool night air; fortunately it wasn't raining and the breeze had died down. A few stars twinkled.

"Isn't it odd," Peggy said, "that we both had just one child?" She paused, but Jan said nothing. "What was *your* reason?"

"You were enough, I guess."

"I was enough? What does *that* mean?"

Jan sighed. "Criminy, Peggy. It doesn't mean a thing."

They walked the rest of the way in silence. It would have been nice, Peggy thought, if her mother had said something tender, or at least shown a little interest in the conversation. But that wasn't her way, never had been. Not that she'd been remiss as a provider; she just wasn't big on showing affection. Peggy's father had been the demonstrative one, freely giving hugs and praise, making up pet names that made his daughter laugh.

Peggy considered her own child. Ben was 31 now and living in San Diego, where he designed "green homes" and lived with a man named Tyler, to whom he was married. Which was fine. She had no problem with that, and neither did Philip. Ben was a sweet boy, everyone said so—you couldn't do better than that. And yes, she reflected now, Ben had been enough. Which was one thing, at least, that she and her mother had in common.

*

When they walked into the hotel lobby, a young man at the desk looked up at them and smiled. "Have a nice evening," he said. Jan paused and started to say something, but the words didn't come, and after a few seconds she closed her mouth and simply smiled at him.

"Thank you," Peggy said. "You too." She and Jan got on the elevator, and Peggy murmured, "It's okay, mom. It's no big deal." Jan did not look up.

"Do you need anything?" Peggy asked when they reached their rooms.

"I'm fine," said Jan. She pushed her card through the lock and over her shoulder said, "Sleep well, dear."

Peggy walked into her room and leaned back against the door for a moment. How strange. How strange that her mother could say that just now, yet not be able to answer the desk clerk. It happened most often, she realized, with strangers, though Jan had never been a shy woman—quiet, yes, but never shy.

Peggy felt tears welling up. What must her mother be thinking right now? She pictured her sitting on the edge of the bed, eyes open wide. Horrible, Peggy thought. Horrible to be a victim of your own mind, to sit there wondering when it would strand you and for how long.

An hour later, when she was watching TV, Peggy's stomach began to bother her—the butter sauce, foreign fish? There was no way of knowing what would give her trouble these days. The episodes were frequent now and made her feel old.

Incredibly, she'd forgotten to pack Tums—maybe her mother had something in her purse. She picked up the phone and called her room, but there was no answer. Was she in the bathroom? Peggy waited five minutes and called again, let the phone ring several times.

Alarmed, she hurried out of the room and knocked on Jan's door. No answer. This made no sense; her mother was a night owl, and even more so as she'd gotten older.

Okay. She would go downstairs to see if desk clerk had seen her. If not, she'd get him to open up the room. Heart beating wildly, Peggy took the elevator to the lobby and was on her way to the front desk when she heard a piano. She looked to the right and saw the etched glass doors to the lounge. Peggy paused a second, then strode across the carpet and entered the bar. There was just a handful of people enjoying the music, and she saw her mother right away: a small slight woman with a silver ponytail, lightly tapping her foot to a lively rendition of "I've Got You Under My Skin." She was sitting alone, and there was a drink, another Manhattan, in front of her.

Peggy's first thought was to join her, but she stopped herself. If her mother had wanted company, she would have asked for it.

The desk clerk gave her a small package of antacids and said he hoped she felt better soon. Riding the elevator, Peggy smiled to herself, glad to give her mother this unexpected pleasure. Jan had frowned on their staying in such an expensive hotel, and it was true they would have been perfectly comfortable somewhere cheaper, but you don't find pianists at Motel 8.

*

Manatee Gardens had a tidy office with cream-colored walls and sturdy blue awnings. There were no trapped reptiles inside, as Peggy had imagined, but there was a beautiful aquarium containing all sorts of flamboyant marine life. Peggy was glad she'd made reservations, as the 6:15 tour was filled to capacity. There were three covered pontoon boats, each designed for twelve guests.

The video was short and informative. The trip to the dive area would take ten minutes, and they would be snorkeling in about ten feet of water. In-water tour guides would be photographing the highlights of the experience, and a CD of these photos would be available for purchase. There were basic rules to follow regarding behavior in the water. Guests were NEVER to chase or crowd a manatee, or come between a mother and calf. Interrupting a sleeping or feeding manatee was forbidden, as was excessive splashing and noise. Guests were instructed to float on the surface and avoid dangling their feet and stirring up the bottom, and if they did get to touch a manatee they could only do so with one open hand. Personal wetsuits could be used, but scuba gear was prohibited as manatees were bothered by bubbles. Extra wetsuits could be found onboard in case those who declined them changed their minds. Jan nodded here and there as they watched the video; she had already seen it, she whispered, online.

Peggy and Jan were assigned to the first boat, along with four children, one teenage girl, two young mothers, two middle-aged women, and an obese, bald man—he and Peggy were the only ones who refused the snorkeling gear. The rest of them tugged on the blue and black wetsuits provided by the staff, and were then handed flippers and snorkels, which they carried outside to the dock. Jan had to be fitted with a child's size suit, and though getting into it had not been easy for her, she was beaming the whole time. Peggy, walking behind her to the boats, snapped a few photos for Philip.

Captain Mike, the bearded, sandy-haired skipper in charge of their group, helped each of them onto the boat. It was still dark and chilly when they boarded, and Peggy was glad for the vinyl covering, through which she could see the moving lights of other boats and a string of brightness along the shoreline. The children were talking and giggling; the two older women were murmuring to one another, sharing comforting banalities.

Dawn broke just as they arrived at the swim site, as if this perfect timing was another detail that Manatee Gardens had carefully considered. To the east, above the dark ridge of trees, the glowing red top of the sun appeared.

"Remember, get into the water slowly," said Captain Mike. "No splashing. Let the manatees come to you."

"Where are they?" the fat man asked.

"They're down there. You'll be able to see them in a few minutes." Holding his camera, the man peered down at the water and waited.

"Oh my," said Jan, who was pulling on her flippers. She sat up and put her mask on, then looked through it at Peggy. The sight of her mother's face in those big goggles with the blue tube sticking up, made her laugh.

Sure enough, within minutes they could see into the water, could make out the sandy bottom, strewn with shells and patches of seaweed, and what they gradually began to recognize as the massive bodies of manatees, not just two or three, but a logjam of them, all hovering above the sand, their backs crusted with barnacles.

Peggy turned to Captain Mike. "How did you know they were here?"

"Secret powers," he said with a wink.

The manatees moved slowly and with odd grace, adjusting their positions with flippers that seemed too small for the job. Their fat, oblong bodies tapered to large flat paddles instead of the legs you expected to find. They looked wrong, Peggy thought, a species on the way to oblivion, unwitting, slow-moving giants not built for the world above them, the jet skis and power boats they could neither see nor avoid. They were doomed, Peggy concluded; all the coddling they required proved it.

The first one off the boat was Toby, Captain Mike's helper, who was there to take pictures and make sure no one swam too far or ran into trouble. One by one, the guests followed him into the water. Jan slipped in like a butter knife, no splash at all. She gave Peggy a thumb's up, then began making her way around the boat, her silver ponytail trailing over her back. The four children streamed off like fish. The middle-aged women, who carried extra weight, bobbed at the surface, their fat making them buoyant.

One of the young mothers, unnerved by the size of the creatures, climbed back onto the boat after just a few minutes. Jan, on the other hand, hung in the water above a trio of manatees twice her length and several times wider. Peggy watched with apprehension, thinking about Steve Irwin and the unpredictability of wild things. What if her presence annoyed them? What if they rose up and knocked her? One little bump could crack a bone.

"Do they ever injure people?" she asked the captain. "Even unintentionally?"

He shook his head. "No ma'am. If you're gentle with them, they're gentle with you."

Peggy nodded slowly, figuring these tours had to be safe, given the potential liability.

The air was warmer now and drenched with life. Sunlight flashed on the water, and more boats could be seen moving over the bay: catamarans and pontoons, slender kayaks nosing into the tributaries. Along the tree-lined shore, streamers of lichen hung off the cypress branches and dipped into the water. Off to the right she saw a buoy that read: Closed Area – Manatee Sanctuary. They had been warned about these areas; you couldn't boat, swim, dive or fish in them. People were trying, Peggy thought, doing what they could to make up for themselves. Her gaze swept across the expanse of water, from one end of King's Bay to the other. What a lovely place it was, with the light green water and brightly colored kayaks. It was like something out of a fairy tale, all the little islands and inlets, and just a few feet below, at our mercy, those huge improbable beasts.

When Peggy looked back at her mother, she saw her face to face with a manatee, its whiskered snout nosing her goggles. Jan placed her open hand on its head, and they stayed that way a moment, before the creature slowly rolled over and offered up its belly, which Jan obligingly stroked. It was a communion beyond words, simply a way of being in the world, as honestly as anyone could be.

Language was often the first to go, Philip had said. In time, Jan's memory would fail, would start to break apart.

But not today. Today she was safe. They all were.

Peggy walked up to the captain. "I want to swim," she said.

Savages

The savages are waiting; they know I'm outside the door. Some I will feed, others I won't. It's not like dinner arrives with any predictability in the wild. This way they stay keen and ready, like nature intended.

The carnivorous plants I tend live in a long narrow room with glass on one side, and I control everything they need: light, temperature, food, water. I keep a close eye on each of them and can usually save the ones that get sick. I'm a better mother than most.

*

My mother gave me a feeble name, Carol Ann Walker, which I changed. I wanted something distinctive, with no ties or tracks, so I opened an atlas and let my finger fall on a town in West Africa called Masso. That sounded fine. My first name, "Kinra," I pulled out of the air. Kinra Masso. Try figuring that one out. You're stuck with your genes, but your name is a wildcard.

No, I am not pretty. My eyes are too small and I don't have much of a chin. What I have too much of are hips—I have those freakishly wide hips some women are cursed with; otherwise I am normal and not fat at all. I don't use make-up because it's a lie, but I do keep my clothes and body clean—there was a time when I couldn't.

Aside from cold wet weather, that's what I minded most about living on the street. Sometimes, when I'm in my bathtub or sitting on my toilet, I remember when I didn't have either, when I took care of my business in Safeway restrooms, filling a plastic water bottle with hand soap on my way out. With a cardboard roof over your head you get canny in a hurry; you see that most everything has value, especially the people you spend your days and nights with. Sharing is how you stay alive.

We were all towing trouble. Some had been displaced by bad luck; others lived on the fringe by choice, preferring privation to whatever hell they came from. A few had lost their sanity, which reminded the rest of us how close that world was. We were cells of the same body, old and young and in-between. When we looked at each other, we saw ourselves.

I don't have friends like that anymore.

*

What separates meat-eating plants from other plants is the ability to digest. Methods of capturing a meal depend on the variety. Pitcher plants sit there with gaping mouths. Sundews ooze goo. Venus fly traps attack. Their teeth-rimmed lobes snap shut, and the world becomes a green tomb for the luckless bug inside. The terror thrills me every time.

Most plants move constantly, their stems twisting and turning, their blossoms opening and closing, but these changes happen slowly, beyond detection. Venus fly traps strike, *commit murder*, right before your eyes—you can understand why kids can't resist them. Not that I approve of children toying with these plants, tormenting them with pencil tips and dead house flies (individual traps—a plant makes several—can close and reopen only seven times before they die, and only three times if they actually digest something). Deadly though they are, Venus fly traps fight for their lives like everything else.

From their strange looks and behavior, you might think Venus fly traps are found in steamy, perilous jungles south of the equator. In fact they are native to North America, the Carolinas specifically, where they flourish on the coastal plains—sunny wet savannahs or pine-studded grasslands. Of course we are robbing their habitat, draining the wetlands to harvest lumber and throw up more houses.

Preventing naturally occurring brush fires is another of our blunders: fly traps are choked out by thick scrub and need the fires to give them room.

Why are we here? Seriously. Why were we ever allowed access?

*

My brother Matt died surfing, smacked in the head by his board. Hollowed out by the death of his only son, my father was unreachable, distant as the moon. When that phase ended, I wished he'd never come back to earth. He started drinking then, steadily and on purpose, and one night he slapped me around just for the hell of it: I wasn't pretty, I wasn't Matt. My father never liked me, only faked it when others were around, and after Matt's death, he stopped pretending and just said whatever hateful thing came into his mind. He was mean to my mother, too, sneered at everything she tried to do for him. One morning he shoved aside the breakfast she'd cooked and said her food make him sick, that *she* made him sick, and then he stomped out of the house. I walked into the kitchen and found her huddled in her chair, shoulders heaving. "Leave him," I said. She looked up and gave me this stricken look; it was clear I was my own. She loved me, I knew that, but love without teeth is no help at all.

I couldn't talk about Matt, or write his name, or look at pictures of him, or go anywhere near his room. My mother reacted differently. For hours at a time, she would lie in his bed. This amazed me, how someone who didn't have the nerve to leave a rotten marriage could be so brave.

*

Venus fly traps are precise. It takes just the right trigger to close up a trap and just the right insect—too small and they slip through, too big and the trap, unable to close, leaks bacteria and poisons itself. Large ants or tiny crickets work well, spiders too. The victims don't have to be alive, but a bug that struggles is more easily digested.

Fly traps don't need to eat; they absorb everything they require from the sun. Their snares are an add-on, insurance perhaps, in place if need be; or maybe a reward system that benefits the achievers, the ones who bother to use what they were given. The plants that don't eat look fine, but you should see the difference a meal or two makes. The fed plants are not only greener and bushier, they hold their leaves higher. They move when my back is turned; when I face them again, their traps are wide open and canted toward me. They would speak if they could, and what they would say is: "More."

*

My father laid into me a second time, shoved me hard on his way to the bathroom. I banged my head against the wall and saw stars. He stopped and looked at me, his face red, his eyes like cinders. I thought he was going to hit me, but instead he staggered back a couple steps and started to cry. Disgusted, I brushed past him and locked myself in my room. I could hear him in the hallway, blubbering apologies, and then I heard my mother, who was crying too. I just kept shoving clothes into my backpack, and as soon as those two sad sacks went to bed I got away.

*

So this is what happens when a Venus fly trap gets sprung. The bug, usually an ant, smells the nectar and hikes up to a trap (in her shrewd way, nature spares the pollinators, who cruise past without interest). If the ant brushes two of those white hairs on the edge, or one hair twice in twenty seconds, the trap swiftly closes—in fact, it changes shape. An electrical current runs through the two lobes, and the cells on the outer walls lengthen, doubling their size in less than a second. The convex lobes turn concave, and the teeth at the top intermesh. The struggling ant stimulates the trigger hairs even further, and soon the lobes are pressed tight and the trap seals itself. Glands on the inside of the lobes begin to secrete digestive juices, drowning the victim.

It takes a week or so for the flytrap to digest its prey. When the trap reopens, all that's left of the insect is a dry exoskeleton. Spiders, lured by this crusty morsel, often become the second course.

When I think about the planning involved, from the eager ant to the unwitting spider, I get goose bumps. I wonder what I'm walking around with, what components I'm not using. Then I wonder who's pulling my strings.

*

Some folks live out their lives on the street, scabbed over with skin cancers, blinded by cataracts, hobbling along on ruined knees. It's surprising how many afflictions you can carry. When you have your health, you have everything, the saying goes. Not really. Health, beauty, those are extras; you can live without them; you can even be happy, or close to it. You're not alone, that's for sure.

I stayed on the streets of East L.A. for 18 months. It wasn't awful. The weather was mostly tolerable, and there were quite a few places to get at least one decent meal a day. I spent a lot of time in libraries, and the churches were a comfort, too. Sometimes they let us sleep on the pews. I remember waking up in the middle of the night, scared at first, and then I'd see the stained glass windows, the light coming through the saints and angels, and my heart would slow down. You don't have to be Catholic to love those windows.

One morning when I was picking cans and bottles out of a nightclub dumpster, I noticed the owner, who was fat and sweaty, hauling out trash cans and rubber mats. I walked right up to him and asked if I could help him, and he frowned at me and shook his head. I didn't blame him—my hair wasn't clean that day, and I was wearing clothes that didn't fit me from a Goodwill drop box. But I kept at it, told him I'd hose off the mats and swab the bar floor and clean the toilets, whatever he needed, and he finally said okay. He gave me a little cash each Friday and let me sleep on a Naugahyde bench in the poolroom, and not once did he try anything creepy. In a few weeks, I was able to buy some new underwear and two decent outfits, which is how I got the job at Milo's Diner. Tammy, the other waitress at Milo's, told me I could rent a room in the house she was living in. It was a crummy house in Glendale, and nothing worked right, and you had to pass through the cubby I slept in to get to the bathroom, but I was fine with it. I had a bed, a real roof and an address. There were four of us in that house, all women, and we all waited table. I really wanted to be a cocktail waitress—they make gobs of money—but you need to be pretty for that.

*

People and animals begin with an egg. What I love about plants is that you can start one from seed or scrap—scraps are faster and more fun. You just pull off a leaf, set it on a bed of sand and peat, put a pinch of soil on the base and keep it moist. In two years you'll have a full-grown plant, whereas a fly trap born from seed takes about five years to mature. I use both methods, and right now I have a total of 184 plants, some of which are ready for division, which is another way my collection grows.

They are not identical. Some are all red, some have red traps, some are saw-toothed. These variations can occur naturally or breeders can coax them into being. I've bought some nice specimens from a nursery near here, but I am not much interested in raising cultivars; my focus is quantity. Besides, whatever odd features I coddle here will be winnowed out in the wild. Left to their own devices, plants always revert to their robust origins. That's why you see variegated plants turning green again; the white parts can't make chlorophyll and are shouldered out.

Venus fly traps must be kept wet, and any black leaves should be trimmed off—that's all the care they require. They can go without food, or you can give them a bug now and then. *Never* fertilize. Most plants use their roots to suck up nutrients from the soil; fly traps live in wet sand and use their roots as anchors. They have no idea what to do with food that comes from beneath them, a meal that doesn't thrash. Still, I give them new medium each spring—equal parts sand and peat—to keep their lives fresh. It's a serious task. Each four-inch pot must be inverted and refilled, and while I am doing this with my right hand, the fly traps wait upside-down in my left hand. I take great care with this event, and I am sure the plants trust me.

*

Working breakfast and lunch at Milo's left my evenings free, and I spent most of them at the Central Library. First I was studying for my GED (a breeze, by the way), then I moved into the natural sciences, which is when I learned about carnivorous plants and other strange things. I read a lot of books about viruses and bacteria, the plagues we miss by a hair's breadth (or not). We fight back with our pills and shots, but nature catches up: Vaccines are hurdles she thrives on.

Some folks believe we'll be swamped by melting ice caps; some think rampant pollution will do us in; others say a maniac will pull the trigger and we'll bomb ourselves into oblivion. I say a microbe will get here first—we'll scarcely know what hit us. A few people may be left standing, subsets with lucky genes and a big responsibility. I'd like to think the wise will be spared—they are rare enough—but nature doesn't work that way.

*

Each year on Halloween I put the savages to sleep. It doesn't take much. I lower the humidifier a notch and pull a gray mesh shade over the windows so no bright sun comes in. Beyond keeping the water trays filled, there is nothing the plants need from me in the cold months. I always miss our time together and can hardly wait till Valentine's Day, when I wake them up again.

When fly traps go into dormancy all their summer leaves go black and are replaced by smaller, low-growing traps. This feral clump—just a waiting set of teeth—is what gets them through the winter. They don't eat during this period and will ignore any meal you offer. Imagine knowing yourself that well.

*

When I was homeless I used to walk up to telephone poles and study the photos of missing persons. My face was never there—not that I expected it to be. I knew my father wouldn't bother, and I doubted my mother had the gumption to go after me like that.

They're useless anyway, those photos. I could look at one and never realize I'd just shared a sandwich or gotten a haircut from that person. Minus certain amenities, people's looks change in a hurry. Men grow beards, and women, without make-up and hair color, are also hard to spot. Bodies change, too. A lot.

You can't tell that your body is adapting—it does that without you. One day you notice your nails are thicker, your skin tougher, your calves more firm than they've ever been; even your night vision becomes sharper.

Oh—and your periods stop. Most of the women I knew back then had stopped menstruating. It was as if nature, seeing we were not equipped for motherhood, had taken away the option. Considering the mess and expense involved in fertility, we were grateful.

*

Have you heard of tissue culture? It's a way of creating quantities of plants, cheaply and quickly, in a sterile environment. Many people collect carnivorous plants, and without tissue culture, there would not be enough plants to go around. There's nothing natural about making plants in beakers, but it does discourage poaching. There's a $50,000 fine for digging up fly traps in North Carolina or collecting their seeds. That's how scant they've become.

*

I was tired of L.A. I had lived there 21 years, and every day it looked the same, a dirty playground stretching in all directions. I didn't think the city had anything left to teach me, and staying on seemed lazy.

I had heard some nice things about Northern California, that it was nothing like the southern half of the state, so I found a *Frommer's* guide and started looking at pictures. For sure, there were more hills and vineyards in the north, and the beaches looked mostly empty. I did not quite believe the blue perfection of Lake Tahoe—were the photos retouched?—or the proportions of a giant redwood looming behind a thimble-sized man. But what charmed me most was a photograph of Jenner Beach, where the Russian River meets the Pacific. There were sloping cliffs on either side dotted with yellow flowers and feathery stands of pampas grass, and sea lions were stacked along the shore like sodden logs, and sun spilled down on the whole scene, spangling the river and ocean. Everything looked exactly as it should, even the man and woman walking on the shoreline, a dog trotting beside them, and that big green river pouring itself into the sea. Surrender, that's what it looked like. Eternal surrender.

I changed my name to Kinra Masso, bought a used Corolla, worked my last lunch at Milo's and headed north. For a couple hours I kept checking the rearview mirror, as if I had stolen something and gotten away with it, but that was just freedom settling in.

I wound up in Guerneville, a town covered in redwoods just fourteen miles from Jenner Beach. First I found a cottage to rent, a damp little place that came with a greenhouse in which the owner had tried and failed to grow tomatoes. I scrubbed it clean and cut down the over-hanging branches, then started ordering trays and pots. There was never any question of what I would grow there.

I also got the job I wanted, a job with a future. If you think being a Safeway cashier doesn't sound like much, you have no idea what unions can do.

*

I miss Matt as much now as I did when he died, but these days I let myself think about him. I feel closest to him in the dark, with no hard facts around. Sometimes I lie in bed and conjure his image, and for a second I can see him clearly, his face a fleeting hope. "Matthew Curtis Walker" I say out loud, to make his name matter still.

I've seen my mother three times since I ran away. The first time she didn't know it; I watched her from our backyard, after dark. She was making dinner, a pot roast, I think.

The second time was right before I moved up to Guerneville. I wanted to come clean, to be done with the secrets and the drama. Out of respect, I called first. I thought I'd give my father the opportunity to clear out, and he did, which pretty much answered the question of whether he was still an asshole. Being with my mother again was just what I expected: hugs and tears and long, helpless looks. We both apologized, for what it was worth, and then we sat there.

The last time I saw her was after my father's funeral—I knew he wouldn't want me there so I didn't go. My mother was thin and listless. I tried to talk her into spending some time with me here, maybe even moving up this way, but she looked at me like I had asked her to spend the rest of her life on the International Space Station.

*

Next month, when the savages are still sleeping, I'm going to rent a box van and take them across country. When we reach the boggy plains of North Carolina, near Wilmington, I will take a spade and plant each one, letting the water flow in and claim them.

It makes me smile already, thinking about those fly traps and what they have in store. When they wake up in the spring they'll be right where they belong. They will know it in an instant

Nine Glorious Days

"Look at that," Ben said, needlessly pointing out the window. "They go on and on and on."

Maggie leaned across him and peered down at the sea of jagged white peaks. "Beautiful," she nodded.

He turned to her, his face radiant. "The Alps!" On his breath she could smell the mushroom omelet he'd had for breakfast. They had flown straight through the night and the blue shadow of his beard was just coming on. His upper lip was chapped; a small line of blood had dried on his chin. She placed her hand on his arm and forced a smile. A moment later the mountains vanished and the land turned into a flat patchwork of green fields and water.

"It looks flooded down there," he said.

Maggie's head ached and an odd pain had developed in her left ear. Once again her gaze moved from the orange seatbelt sign, to the air phone (such a temptation), to the laminated flight information, and finally to the lumpy turquoise sweater growing in the lap of the woman beside her. The woman had not spoken a word, had done nothing but knit—click-click, click-click—ever since they left New York. Across the aisle, hunched beneath a blanket, a man snored steadily.

"That's the landing gear," said Ben when they heard a high-pitched whirring.

"Thank god," Maggie sighed. "I can't wait to get off this plane. My shoulders feel like somebody poured cement in them."

He looked at her, his face solicitous. "It was a good flight, though, don't you think? Not much turbulence."

This was their first trip abroad. To celebrate the year 2000, the turn of the millennium, Ben had decided that they would finally visit Italy, the birthplace of his forebears. Determined that everything

46

would be splendid, he had spent months reading guidebooks and talking with travel agents, methodically plotting a nine-day tour. He knew precisely which trains they would take, what sights they would see and where they would sleep each night. She didn't care about the lodging, Maggie had stated, so long as they had their own bathroom.

It was impressive, the lengths he had gone to, buying security wallets and electrical adaptors, studying the customs, learning the language. Each morning for the past several weeks she had heard him talking to the bathroom mirror: *"Mi chiamo* Ben. *Come si chiama?"* At his encouragement Maggie had memorized a few words herself, though she didn't have much faith in them. How could they stake their survival on a handful of chummy phrases?

They could never let down their guard, that's what she'd been told. Big cities were the worst: corrupt shopkeepers; berserk drivers; smiling, treacherous children. One wrong move could cost them dearly. She had tried to explain this to Ben, but the subject only irritated him: "You see what you're doing? You're setting us up. You go over there looking for trouble and you're going to find it."

He had a point of course. This was not the first time they had argued about her dark prophecies. But didn't it work the other way as well? Didn't Ben, with his ceaseless faith, burden himself unduly? Nine glorious days, he promised. That, Maggie thought, was a lot of pressure.

When they got off the plane, four yellow buses were waiting. No announcements were made; the passengers simply boarded the shuttles, like cattle or prisoners, in a dumb, orderly fashion. There were no seats; everyone hung onto the bars and peered over each other's shoulders, trying to see where they were going.

"Pretty slick operation," Ben observed, as their shuttle lurched to a stop. The doors opened and people began spilling onto the tarmac. Maggie took hold of Ben's arm and they walked, a little wobbly, into the airport. It was a toy-like structure with brightly colored beams and girders, containing one large room and a few self-explanatory booths. They exchanged their dollars for lire, then bought two bus tickets to Milan.

"Isn't this easy?" Ben said, beaming. "Now *this* is the way to run an airport."

Maggie eyed the two policemen who were strolling through the room, armed with guns and a German shepherd. "It's no nonsense alright." The men unnerved her with their swaggering authority, their gleaming weapons, their thin hard smiles. They spoke only to each other, not even bothering to look at the dog as it nosed its way through passengers and luggage. Maggie froze when the men approached her and Ben. "Screw you," she whispered as they walked away.

The ride to Milan would take 45 minutes, Ben informed her, and the train to Florence was just over two and a half hours. Maggie ignored these facts and peered out the clouded window of the bus.

"It's nothing like I imagined," she said as they passed a row of industrial buildings.

"You're probably thinking of Tuscany. This region isn't like that."

"We're staying in Tuscany, right?"

Ben nodded. "And Umbria and Latium."

The pain in her ear was more noticeable now. If it became constant, if it felt hot, those would be signs of an infection.

"Florence first," Ben went on, "then Siena, Orvieto and Rome."

"What about Venice? Can't we squeeze in Venice?"

"Venice is in northern Italy. We won't be anywhere near it, not this time." He smiled and patted her knee. "We can't see everything in one trip."

"I suppose not," she said. Ben turned back to the window and Maggie frowned. It had taken them nearly half a century to get here. When would they be back?

*

Back in Sacramento their daughter Helen was taking care of the cats and fish, hopefully the houseplants. This was not the original plan. Helen and her husband Jake were supposed to be traveling with them. Maggie wasn't sure if Helen had been deterred by the winding steps and steep stone streets of Italy, or if, presented with enough new challenges in her own country, she'd lost interest in world travel. In any case, Helen had said no and Jake didn't argue, and that's when Maggie felt her own enthusiasm collapse. All those gay scenes in her mind—the four of them sipping Campari, dining on rooftops, gazing at golden towers—they were all sucked away.

Eighteen months before, on a bright and breezy morning, Helen was riding her motorcycle on a country road. There was a curve in the road and she didn't see the fallen tree until it was too late. She broke three ribs and lost her leg.

At least she was alive, friends had said, at least it wasn't a head injury. One had gone so far as to say that Helen might be spiritually enriched by the experience; it was all Maggie could do to keep from striking her.

Helen never railed against her fate. After two weeks of shocked silence she emerged grim and determined. Her wound healed faster than expected, and her arms grew strong and shapely as she vaulted through space on her crutches.

Sometimes, in those first few weeks, Maggie forgot how to breathe. She would think of her daughter's ruined body and she would start to gasp. She would fall asleep and wake up choking. It wasn't just the physical impairment, the things that Helen could no longer do, it was the injury to her womanhood. A man could get away with such a loss, but a woman was undone. "Imagine it," Maggie had ranted, drunkenly, to Ben. "She'll never feel desirable, ever again."

As if he didn't know this. He still couldn't bear to look at Helen's prosthetic leg, and he had cried the first time he saw her walking on it. Maggie had cupped Ben's face in her hands and reminded him that the crutches were exhausting and cumbersome, and he said it was just that Helen looked so strong when she used them, like an athlete. He hated seeing her limp on that plastic leg, hated the thought of her buckling it on each day.

They didn't share their grief anymore—it hadn't helped. Now when they spoke of Helen they offered each other only blithe reassurances, bland and safe as samplers. Their words were like smooth stones skipping over deep dark water.

*

Ben was going on about the train, and how fast and quiet it was, and why didn't they make trains like this in the States.

Maggie looked at him askance. *The States?*

"And that station in Milan—wasn't that incredible?"

Maggie reflected. "It reminded me of a casino."

"A casino!"

"Yes, Ben. A casino." She turned to the window and squinted up at the pale sky. "Have you noticed that the light is different here? It feels like it should be late afternoon." She closed her eyes. "Jesus, I'm tired."

Ben pulled a pen from his pocket and made some calculations in his new spiral notebook. "Well, by the time we get to Florence we will have been traveling 26 hours."

Maggie studied her husband. His beard was very noticeable now but the rest of his face was nearly as pale as his windbreaker. In this stark light everything about him appeared older. Under his thinning hair she could just make out the shape of his skull. His nose was definitely bigger and his upper lip was beginning to shrink. She did not want to imagine how she looked at this moment.

"Why didn't we just fly into Florence?" Maggie said.

"I told you. There aren't any direct flights from New York to Florence." He gestured at the scenery. "But this way we get to see more of the countryside."

Which was far from inspiring. It was flat, for one thing, and the trees, most still bare, held their network of black branches against a pallid sky. Here and there low-slung vacant buildings, painted ochre or dull orange or muddy pink, squatted on the landscape.

"How long till we get to Florence?" she said.

Ben checked his watch. "Twelve minutes."

"And how far is our hotel from the station."

"A few blocks—walking distance." She looked at him incredulously. "We can take a cab, though." He stretched his arms out in front of him and grinned through a yawn. "I can't believe we're in Italy, can you? I thought we'd see the Duomo and the Bell Tower this afternoon, and then have dinner at a pizzeria near the hotel—it's a Frommer's favorite."

Maggie shook her head. "I am not doing any sightseeing this afternoon. Can't we just relax for five minutes?"

Ben's face fell.

"I know, I know. There's so much to see and so little time and you've got it all worked out, but I am not going to be rushing around every day like a maniac. And right now I'm exhausted, Ben. I can't even think straight. If I don't lie down soon I'm going to have a goddamn stroke."

Ben nodded slowly; she could tell he was making revisions. "You're right," he said. "We should get some rest. We can see the Duomo in the morning, when it opens."

Maggie brought her hands to her temples and began massaging them. Her head still throbbed but the pain in her ear, she noticed now, was gone. Heartened, she squeezed her husband's leg.

"We can still go to that pizza place tonight. We need a decent meal. What does Frommer's say about it?"

This was a travel day; it really didn't count. Italy, she and Ben—they would all be better tomorrow.

*

There was a big kitchen store in Florence, Ben had told her on the flight. High-end. Lots of hand-painted dishes. "Mmmm," Maggie replied without interest. Ben still assumed, like everyone else, that because she sold culinary supplies she was enamored of them. The truth was, she was sick to death of tart pans, ring molds and precious platters.

She had entered the business by default—who aspires to be a peddler of kitchenware? Not many people knew this, but she had wasted a lot of money pursuing an education in psychology. For two and a half years she had worked for the state, trying to help troubled teens. When one of them pushed her into a parked school bus and dislocated her shoulder, she collected disability for six months and then attempted private practice. This was worse. These children were ostensibly normal. It wasn't until you got them alone that you learned, bit by bit, the cruelties they were capable of, the random, vicious ways they took their revenge. Mostly they were beyond her help. And the stories she was stuck with, all those odious images she had to bring home, into her living room, into her bed.

She simply hadn't the hide for it. There was nothing to do but cut her losses and close up shop. In a last ditch effort to justify her diploma she took a job as a high school counselor, and while the work was more palatable she had never felt so useless, there in that foolish cubicle, trying to steer contemptuous teens toward a future they wouldn't regret.

At least there was a measure of gratification in what she did now. People sought her out, took her advice. It wasn't easy either, keeping current on all the paraphernalia you could cram in a kitchen these days. While her customers didn't need half the stuff they bought, she could hardly be accused of coercing them. People came to The Gourmet Chef with their checkbooks wide open, convinced that a set of French butter molds was going to make a difference in their lives. The hours were good, the commissions adequate, and if Maggie wearied of the frivolous merchandise, the silly, privileged patrons, she had only to recall her first career.

*

Wide awake on the hard mattress, Maggie listened to the other guests tromping down the halls and stairways, their shoes striking the marble floors. Why not throw down some carpet, she fumed, recalling the plush corridors of the Best Westerns back home. Then the rushing of water through pipes as showers and toilets went on and off. And after that, after every last tourist had tucked himself into bed, a couple across the alleyway began to have noisy sex, the girl's dramatic ohs and ahs resounding through the Florentine night, until the boy—Maggie assumed it was a boy—finished with a grunt.

Through all the ruckus Ben slumbered on. He could do that, could fall asleep at will. And his dreams! If only, if just for a night, she could dream like Ben. He flew, he told her, with his arms stretched out like wings, nice and slow, over valleys and rivers. He fished for bright blue marlin, sailed yachts across the Caribbean. The joyous feats, the things he would never be or do or have, came to him in sleep.

It wasn't fair. Didn't she deserve equal treatment? Hadn't she labored long, suffered sufficiently? What would it hurt to throw a few sweet dreams her way?

In the center of her chest Maggie felt a rising pressure. She turned her attention to her left arm—no pain there. But she did feel queasy, almost nauseous, and her abdomen was swollen. It was probably the antipasto plate: those glistening ribbons of fat-streaked prosciutto, the peppered black olives drowned in oil. They had a salad after that, some mixed lettuces with sliced tomato, which they had to dress themselves. Ben got a kick out of drizzling on his own green oil and cloudy vinegar, but Maggie complained that you couldn't mix it properly. The pizza was even stranger. Instead of distributing the artichoke hearts, mushrooms and olives, the cook had placed them in neat little piles so that you had to dismantle the whole thing before you ate it. The *vino della casa* was another disappointment, though after the first carafe Maggie stopped caring. Ben had warned her that Italian house wines would seem very mild compared to California varietals and he was right. "Toddlers could drink this stuff," Maggie said, polishing off her third glass. "I think they do," he told her.

Maggie's stomach rumbled ominously. Flipping back the covers, she got to her feet, padded into the bathroom and snapped on the light switch. For several seconds she fished through her nylon sack of cures and cosmetics, and then, provoked, she dumped the contents onto the terra cotta floor. A bottle of ibuprofen rolled one way, her eye drops another. There, under a pink-wrapped panty liner, were the Mylanta tablets. She pushed two through their foil backing and quickly chewed them.

Using the opportunity to pee, she sat on the toilet and regarded the bathroom. In front of her was the shower, an ineffectual arrangement consisting of a circular metal rod and a curtain that traversed it. There was a drain underneath and a slight depression in the tiles, but as she had discovered this afternoon, the water simply pooled for a moment, then spilled across the entire floor. On the wall beside the shower hung the towels, large squares of white cotton that looked and felt like tablecloths. Above the tiny sink was an electrical outlet that had shorted out her hair dryer despite the special gadget Ben had installed. Well, what could they expect for the money they were paying? Their rooms would be clean, the travel agent had assured Ben, and they would have private baths, but beyond that he could guarantee nothing.

If this was to be the trip of their lives, Maggie had argued, why not loosen up the purse strings, at least for part of the time: maybe one upscale hotel, three or four swank restaurants, but Ben demurred. The accommodations he had chosen were approved by Frommer's, and wasn't it more fun anyway to experience a few of the cultural quirks? They didn't want a corporate, sanitized version of Italy, they wanted the real thing. As for the food, it was supposed to be rustic, and what they bought at *salumerias* or ordered in *trattorias* would likely be more authentic than the meals they'd find in pricey, heavily touristed *ristorantes*. He had used just those words, smugly employing his new Italian.

While these arguments sounded reasonable, Maggie was not convinced. If Ben had one overriding feature, it was his infuriating thriftiness. He held dire views about their future and the money they would need to stay alive, and so every month after the bills were paid he swept whatever was left into various retirement funds. Maggie had grown to resent this onerous, unquenchable old age that looted their youth and promised nothing. What were they to do with that money while they were nodding off in their rockers? For a few upgrades right now, she would trade one whole dusty year.

*

Church bells. Maggie opened her eyes and listened to the hollow notes as they echoed through the streets. Michelangelo had heard these bells. Leonardo da Vinci. Botticelli. She had just seen a PBS special on Renaissance art. God what a time for geniuses! A tormented artist around every corner, chipping at stone with bloody fingers, painting the long sad faces of saints on an endless procession of frescoes.

Maggie heard the key in the door and looked up expectantly.

"I couldn't get coffee to go," Ben said, coming into the room. "They don't sell it that way. But all the little corner shops are opening now and we can get coffee at any of them. I just had a cappuccino—it was delicious."

"Why don't they sell coffee to go?" she asked, aggrieved by this latest disappointment.

Ben shrugged impatiently. "I don't know, they just don't. It's a good idea, if you ask me. Cuts down on plastics and litter."

"Okay," Maggie muttered. "Okay, I'll get dressed." She went into the bathroom and Ben talked to her through the closed door.

"I took a walk down *Via de Cerchi*, the street to the right of us? The produce vendors are setting up their stalls. Wait till you see the fruit, every color you can imagine, and they arrange it so carefully.

You can't touch it; you have point to what you want."

Maggie, rubbing lotion onto her face, frowned. "How can you tell if it's ripe?"

"Everything's ripe."

*

The morning air was cool and damp. Buildings of stone loomed on both sides of the narrow streets, turning them into tunnels, all of which ended with a glimpse of the green-striped Duomo, massive and inescapable. Already the city was clotted with people, and Vespas kept roaring by, sending everyone up against the brown walls. Maggie felt bad for the dogs who, leashed and wretched, picked their way down the street on stiff little legs. She cast a baleful look at one of the owners. Who would put an animal through this?

"Let's try that one," Ben said, pointing to a store. They crossed at the corner, where the smell of coffee and fresh bread mingled with the warm stench rising from a sewer grate.

An older couple ran the shop, he making coffee and sandwiches, she taking the money. Both were heavy set, their faces creased with age and resignation. Maggie had seen that same sag and slump on most of the local men and women, as if they were functioning collectively, as if at a certain age they all agreed to discard their vanity and merge into obscurity. How different they were from the young Italians who swaggered down the streets in tight black clothes, ignoring everything but each other.

Her cappuccino was served in a pretty yellow cup. She wanted to drink it at one of the tables but Ben shook his head: "Remember what I told you? It costs three times as much if you sit down." "Naturally," she murmured. And so they stood at the bar alongside several other customers, some of whom pointed to a collection of bottles on the wall ("*grappa*," Ben whispered) and demanded a '*caffe coretto.*' This was fascinating, the boredom with which the men doused their cups of espresso, the no-nonsense way they dispatched them. Spiked or straight, there was something seductive, something not quite licit about these miniature coffees, dispensed as they were in potent, measured amounts. And suddenly, as if her own dose had kicked in, Maggie felt buoyant, even reckless. "*Grazie*" she said to the man, sliding her cup back across the counter. Ben wrapped an arm around her shoulders and smiled approvingly.

Halfway up Giotto's Tower Maggie got a stitch in her side and had to rest. Ben, red-faced and breathing heavily, sat on a step and opened his guidebook. Seeing him like this made Maggie nervous. He was a middle-aged man with a desk job. Sudden death would not be remarkable.

"192 steps to go," he panted.

"You've been *counting?*"

"The book might be wrong—I want to see for myself."

She stared at him a moment and then began massaging her side.

"I'm going to need a nap this afternoon," she said. "I still feel like hell."

"You do?" he said, tilting his head sympathetically.

"Don't *you?*" she asked. "You must be feeling some jet lag."

He shrugged. "A little, I guess. I could probably use a nap, too. That's what they do here, that's why the shops close at 1:00." He looked at her hopefully. "I thought we might see the Bargello after this—it's the one with all the statues?"

She did love statues. Horses rearing, men grappling. Frozen struggles.

"Fine with me," Maggie said. She nodded toward the stairs. "Let's take this slow, okay?"

It was worth the climb, they agreed, just to be up this high, in the wind again, clear of the foul air and noisy vehicles. They leaned across the stone ledge and surveyed the red tiled rooftops of Florence. There were trees on the fringes of the city and dark green hills etched on the horizon. Colossal white clouds hung over the landscape.

"Trees," Maggie said with a sigh. She shook her head. "I'd go nuts in this city—it's all stone."

"I guess that's why they have window boxes everywhere." Ben pointed. "Right down there is our hotel. See? That's the *Via del Corso*."

Maggie recognized nothing and then stopped trying to. "Doesn't it surprise you, how big this place is?"

"Yes," Ben said, snapping pictures.

"I didn't like the Duomo," she went on. "I mean, the outside's pretty impressive with all that colored marble, but the inside is so bleak. Those gloomy, awful paintings." She shuddered. "It's such a depressing religion, don't you think?"

Ben aimed the camera at the church's dome. "The Italians are very serious about their faith," he said. "They spent 14 years building the Duomo." He lowered the camera and looked at her. "It was finished in 1434, so it's"—he paused—"566 years old."

Maggie, as always, was impressed. She could not do math in her head, or remember the date a church was finished, or spot their hotel from their air. In peevish, and sometimes idle, moments, she tried to imagine life without her husband: It seemed possible, but risky.

*

A misty rain was falling. They were walking down the *Via dei Neri*, on their way to a restaurant Ben had seen earlier.

"You're right about the shops," Maggie said as they passed another spotless meat market. She eyed the jaunty hanging sausages, the neat rows of olive oil and anchovies. "So picturesque. When I think of all the ratty corner stores back home. Oh god," she said, grabbing Ben's arm. "Look at that!" A stuffed boar's head sat on the counter, snout raised, teeth hooked and yellow.

Ben chuckled. "It gets your attention."

They arrived at the restaurant a little early, but the proprietor, a tall man with a long grey beard, smiled gently and offered them a table and a glass of Chianti.

"I like this place," Maggie said, restored by the wine. It was a small eatery with yellow lights, chipped green walls and old photos of Italians working their fields. From behind a curtain came the rattle of pans, and the seductive odors of wood smoke and roasted meat drifted into the dining room. Maggie ran her hands over the green marble-topped table. "It's quaint."

Ben was concentrating on the menu. "What looks good to you?" he asked.

"Not a full meal," Maggie said. "My stomach's kind of iffy. Maybe just a salad."

"Okay," Ben said. "And how about the crostini?" He pulled out his phrasebook. "Vor-ray-moh," he murmured, "vor-RAY-moh."

"What does that mean?"

"We would like." He slipped the book back in his pocket.

"You look nice tonight," he told her. "You look healthy."

It was the wine of course; it had flushed her cheeks. She did not feel healthy, she felt tired. And *sore*. Her whole body was sore. Was it from the plane? Climbing all those stairs? But she felt this way more often than not. Would she become arthritic? Was it happening already? Wasn't it odd, at 48, to be this stiff?

"So what was your favorite place today?" he asked. "The Bargello?"

Maggie nodded firmly. "Definitely. I liked that big statue of Bacchus. The upper floors weren't as good—the suits of armor, and all those perverted little satyrs with erections. I'm a little tired of looking at penises."

"Uh-oh," Ben said. Maggie, lifting her glass, laughed.

"The Bargello used to be a jail," he said. "They tortured people there. There were hangings out the windows so the public could watch." He leaned across the table and looked at her squarely. "Would *you* have watched?"

"Once," she said. "I'm sure I would have watched once."

It was a good evening, one she would look back on as the high point of their trip. Walking back to the hotel they stopped for gelato, and then they strolled in a falling mist through the *Piazza della Signoria*, where brawny, fearless statues kept watch through the night.

*

When Maggie woke the next morning Ben was sitting in a chair by the window making notes in his spiral binder. His blue travel shirt was wrinkled, though it wasn't supposed to do that, and a tuft of hair was sticking up on his head.

"*Buon giorno*," he said. "Did you sleep okay?"

Maggie struggled to pull herself up against the headboard. "Better than the night before. This bed's awful, though."

"A little while ago you spoke in your sleep. You said, 'Lock the door.' You said it twice."

She reached into her vanishing grab bag of dreams but came up with nothing. "I haven't a clue. Did I sound panicky?"

"Maybe. It was hard to tell." He looked out the window. "Listen to the doves!" A medley of notes sailed into the room, clear and round, as if the birds were blowing their songs through a flute. "Have you ever heard anything like that?" Ben whispered.

Maggie shook her head. "It's pretty. It's like music." She stretched her arms above her head. "What are you doing over there?"

"Figuring out how much we spent yesterday. It's tricky, all these thousands of lire. 20,000 lire is only about $13."

"So what did we spend?"

"$40 on museums, $48 on food and tips. Plus the room, that's another $60. If we're careful about the incidentals, we'll be fine."

Maggie crossed her arms over her chest. "What do you mean by incidentals?"

He capped his pen and looked at her. "Oh, you know, little things—coffee, snacks, souvenirs. That map of Florence cost us six bucks."

"Jesus, Ben. *Coffee? Maps?*" She flipped back the covers and got out of bed. "I'll try to control myself."

*

"'Adoration of the Magi.'" Ben looked at the painting, then back at the booklet in his hand. "There's supposed to be a self-portrait in this one." He peered again at the scene and pointed. "Right there—I think that's Botticelli."

Maggie cocked her head at the painting. "I'm numb. I have no idea what I'm looking at anymore."

Ben read on. "The Botticelli rooms are the highlights of the Uffizi."

"Then we should have seen them first," she said, glancing at her watch. "I'm topped off already."

"Let's try to see a little more. Da Vinci is coming up." They walked on to the next group of people, all clustered in front of 'The Birth of Venus.'

Ben chuckled. "They call this 'Venus on the Half Shell.'"

Which made Maggie think of icy cold oysters—how she'd love a plate of those right now!

"I'm starved," she whispered.

Ben turned to her. "A half hour, okay? We paid a fortune to get in here."

*

They were eating lunch in a park, looking out over a row of shrubs and an empty flower bed. Behind them was a dense tangle of woods. On a hillside to the left men were swinging big hammers, demolishing a stone wall. Ben bit into his sandwich and squinted at the workers.

"They're not wearing eye protection."

Maggie regarded the shaggy hedge and said, "We probably shouldn't be here. I think this place is under construction." From what she had seen, the entire city, from the grimy statues to the fractured *palazzi*, was in the process of being rescued: small, ceaseless measures to stall the ruin of time. Maggie looked at her sandwich. "This is pretty good—it could use some mayonnaise though." She passed her cup to Ben and he poured her more wine.

Maggie gave a deep sigh. "God it's nice to be away from people for five minutes." She squeezed Ben's arm. "Remember those two women at the museum, the docents? How bad they smelled? People don't bathe here like we do."

Ben folded his wax paper and tucked it in the pocket of his windbreaker. "I really didn't notice."

"You're kidding."

He draped his arms across the back of the bench and yawned. A piece of prosciutto was stuck in his teeth. Maggie pointed to her own mouth. "You've got food stuck right there," she said, baring her teeth. He dug a moment with his fingernail. "Gone," she told him.

"The weather's perfect," he said, gazing up at the blanched sky, "almost balmy. I was afraid it would be cold in April." He cleared his throat. "I thought we might see the science museum after this—it's not far from here."

No. Not today. She could not drag herself through another gallery, could not stand before one more spectacle and summon the proper wonder. Admiration, she'd discovered, was exhaustible, and she had spent most of hers at the first stop, gaping at Michelangelo's David. How do you absorb such a thing? How do you know when to move on? That Ben had room for more faintly repelled her.

"You go," she told her husband. "I need to regroup. I think I'll poke around on my own a bit."

She could see the hurt come into his face, though he didn't burden her with it, which was yet another decent thing about him. Instead he got to his feet and handed her the street map of Florence. "Have fun," he said. "I'll see you back at the hotel." Maggie watched him walk away, a slight man in a light blue windbreaker, until he was out of sight and she was alone in the world.

She spent a moment studying the map and then headed back

toward the hotel, past the golden Pitti Palace and the muddy Arno, past the silver jewelers and leather merchants and the windows filled with trendy footwear (how the Italians loved their shoes!). On impulse she stopped at a corner coffee bar. "*Uno espresso*," she said, "*per favore*," and the stern-faced woman took her lire without comment. Sandwiches were stacked on the counter under a plastic cover, and Maggie wondered how long they'd been there and if people ever got sick from bad meat, because come to think of it, there sure was a lot of unrefrigerated pork in this city. What would Helen say about that? She'd have to remember to ask her.

Maggie was the only customer, and it wasn't much fun standing by herself, trying to think of something she knew how to say. She pointed to her little painted cup.

"Bella," she said, smiling.

The owner, a corpulent man with oily, gray-streaked hair, looked up from the espresso machine he was polishing. "*Grazie*," he sighed, turning back to his work. The woman, who stood near the register, arms folded, gave a nod. Where was that famous Italian warmth, those cheery *mama mias* you see on TV?

Back in the hotel room, Maggie peeled off her slacks and blouse and sat on the bed, idly regarding the small purple veins that had bloomed on her thighs. Compared to many women her age she was in pretty good shape, plump around the waist, but who cared? Not Ben. He saw her every morning, with her puffy eyes, her sheet-pleated skin, and he smiled, the same way he had smiled at her for 23 years. Even after Helen's accident, when he could not bear the solace of an embrace, even then he had brightened at the sight of her.

He had never been hard to please, a trait Maggie both scorned and envied. Was the formula as basic as that? Did a life well-lived demand nothing more than a simple and sweeping concurrence? Once, not long after they were married, she asked Ben if he was happy selling cars, and after a moment he said, yes, he supposed he was, and then, warming to the subject, he told her about the psychology of the business and what he had learned about people.

"You always say 'Welcome,'—it reduces their fear. And you ask them if they're first-time customers, so they get a warm feeling about the company.

"I always do what they do," he went on. "They scratch their chin, I scratch my chin; they clear their throat, I do too. But this is the most important thing." He paused and brought his fingertips together. "Never discuss the price until you've sold the car."

Wide-eyed, Maggie listened to every word, amazed at the stealth her husband was capable of, the life he lived quite competently without her.

Naturally he had done well, had moved up from domestic to European models and now sold only "reconditioned" vehicles—luxury cars with hidden pedigrees. Maggie had fantasies of Ben coming home one day in a champagne Mercedes, though she knew he was perfectly happy with their maroon Camry and saw no sense in trading up.

What she wanted right now was a nice tall scotch and soda. Wistfully she thought of the six miniature bottles of Johnnie Walker stowed in her suitcase. Why didn't they have ice machines in these hotels? You couldn't even find a real bar around here, not that it would be open anyhow; these people napped through the cocktail hour.

Uncapping her bottle of spring water she took a swallow. This was better for her anyway. That's what Helen kept telling her. Helen was a dietitian. She knew all sorts of things, like how long it took an egg salad sandwich to move through one's digestive track.

A sudden dull pain assailed her ear. She waited a few seconds and it came again. Probably an infection after all, something she picked up in the mall last week—all those swarming children. She took three ibuprofen and got into bed, pulling the stiff sheets over her.

What if it got bad? She couldn't just let it go. Would the doctors speak English? They would have to, wouldn't they? A few of them? And what about the paperwork? Would that be in English?

The night before they left Sacramento Ben's sister had gone on and on about her trip to Spain and how rejuvenating it was. "There you are," she said, "smack dab in the middle of a brand new world, and you don't pay taxes, and you don't know a soul, and everything around you is something you've never seen." She beamed at Maggie and threw up her hands. "Is there anything more *freeing* than travel?" At the time they had all agreed with her, had lifted their glasses in a toast to adventure.

But it wasn't true. You weren't free at all. You spent twelve cramped hours on a plane, and then you were herded into an airport run by armed police, and when you finally got to your hotel they took your passport and made you keep your room key at the desk, and after that you stumbled around a city where you couldn't speak to anyone or find a restaurant that opened before 7:00 pm, so you ended up back in your hotel room, on a mattress too hard to sleep on, with some scotch you couldn't drink and an earache you prayed wouldn't get worse.

*

The restaurant Ben had chosen was crowded and noisy.

"They just opened," he said as they followed the host to a table. "This is a good sign."

"They're all tourists," Maggie informed him, glancing at the family of Asians next to them.

"The guidebook said not to miss it. The pasta is supposed to be out of this world."

Maggie looked at the menu. "What's *trippa?*"

"Tripe."

"*Vitello?*"

Ben pulled his menu decoder out of his pocket. "Let's see...veal."

"*Agnello?*"

"I know that one. Lamb."

"What a carnivorous bunch."

Ben arched an eyebrow. "And we're not?"

Maggie shrugged. "I don't know. You just see so much of it here. Sausages hanging in your face, and those huge hunks of pork with the fur still on them." She shuddered.

Ben closed his menu. "Well, I think I'll try the *bistecca fiorentina*—it's grilled T-bone, a specialty here. In Florence, I mean. What about you?"

Maggie pushed her menu aside. "Minestrone, I guess." She looked to her left, where a thin man in a white T-shirt was sliding pizzas into an oven. "Jesus Christ," she murmured.

"What?"

"He's smoking. The pizza guy. His cigarette is hanging over the *dough*."

Ben glanced at the man. "Yeah, they're not much concerned with that here."

"Half the people in this room are smoking—it's gross." She turned back to her husband. "You know, for a country so smug about its food, you'd think they'd ban smoking in restaurants."

Ben gave a noncommittal nod.

"I don't think I've had a lungful of fresh air since we climbed the Bell Tower. All those beat-up little cars spewing out smoke. No emission controls *whatsoever*. And they wonder why their statues are deteriorating." A swell of patriotism rose in her. "You know, we may not do everything right, but at least we make an effort to clean up the planet."

Ben covered her hand with his own. "Stop comparing. You're not giving yourself a chance to enjoy anything."

She glared at him. He was right, of course. "Okay," she said, her voice hard and dismissive. "Okay." She took a deep breath, illustrating her self-control. "So. How was the science museum?"

A bored-looking waiter appeared then, and Ben ordered their meal.

"Why are all the waiters men?" Maggie asked when he left.

"I'm not sure, but I know it's a very respected profession here."

"Well there you go," Maggie murmured.

"Anyway," Ben said, "the museum was amazing, just amazing. All these intricate models and instruments—you can't really understand them. They're inventions, mostly, or the beginnings of inventions. Lots of astronomy and physics."

Maggie picked up her bread plate and turned it over, looking for the name of the manufacturer.

"And they had some really weird medical stuff. They had these life-size models—I guess they were made out of wax—of babies in the womb, in all these different positions. But it wasn't just the baby, it was the whole thing, the whole inside of the woman from the waist to the thighs."

Maggie put down the plate. "Good god. What were they for?"

"Training tools, I guess, for the obstetricians."

"Sorry I missed those," Maggie said.

"And the surgical instruments!"

Maggie put up her hand. "That's enough. I'd like to keep my appetite, thank you—such as it is."

"You're not very hungry?"

Maggie shook her head. "I haven't felt right since we got here. And I have this earache thing going on. What do we do, anyway, if we get sick here?"

Ben gave her arm a reassuring tap. "Don't worry, I covered that. I have a list of English-speaking doctors." A smile broke over his face. "Tomorrow we'll be in Siena; they say everyone loves Siena. No cars allowed, by the way."

"Thank god," said Maggie.

The minestrone was appalling: chunks of hard vegetables floating in a watery broth. Maggie nudged the bowl toward Ben.

"Taste this."

He picked up his spoon, took a sip and shrugged. "It's not the best I've had, but it's not bad."

"The vegetables aren't even *cooked!* For god's sake, Ben. You can say it's awful. You are not responsible for this goddamn bowl of soup."

He put down his fork and looked at her wearily. "Stop it. Please."

Shame warmed her cheeks. She reached out and squeezed his hand. "I'm sorry. I really am. I feel strange. I think my period must be coming."

"You just had your period."

"I know. But it feels like hormones."

"Try this," he said, spearing a piece of meat. "It's delicious."

He was right, the smoky flavor was wonderful.

"Very good," she nodded, chewing. And chewing. It was also tough as hell.

*

The clamorous lovebirds were at it again.

"So much for a good night's sleep," Maggie said, rolling onto her back.

"My god," breathed Ben. "What's he doing to her?"

"I'd love to throw a bucket of ice water on those two."

Ben propped himself up on his elbow and brought his lips close to Maggie's ear: "Maybe they're trying to tell us something."

Maggie frowned in the dark. Now *that* was the last thing she felt like doing....but she had been so unpleasant at dinner. With a sigh, she turned onto her side and faced her husband. Who, it turned out, couldn't quite manage the job.

How glad she was not to be a man, everything dependent on that poor dangle of flesh. It was the wine, she supposed—they drank quite a bit at dinner. Or maybe just an age thing, a flagging prostate—most men, she'd read, have that trouble sooner or later. He had felt bad about it of course, and perversely she had let him, had in fact feigned a slight annoyance before offering a few pat words she knew wouldn't assuage him. Eventually he was rescued by sleep, and for a long time after that Maggie stared into the darkness, acquainting herself thoroughly with the monster she had become.

Ben deserved more, she'd be the first to admit it. She had no right to make her husband as wretched as she was.

Helen's accident had devastated them both, but for Ben, who had taught his daughter how to ride a motorcycle, the grief must have been harsher. In those first weeks afterward, he used to roam the house at night, unable to sleep. When he came home after work he hardly spoke, just ate his dinner and retreated. Locked in her own hell, Maggie scarcely noticed. Suffering from the same affliction, they were of no use to each other.

But Ben had managed to emerge. How had he done that? If anything, he had turned kinder, while she had clearly gone the other way, her bitterness running neck and neck with his goodness.

She had seen that decency in him the first time they met, the subtle ways he rescued people, noticing their small embarrassments and swiftly easing them. Maggie wasn't sure just what balance of qualities led to her loving him, but that was surely in the mix. She even considered that marrying such a person would be advantageous, that over time she too might become imbued with tenderness. Obviously she'd been wrong. She could not keep up with Ben and she was tired of trying. What had prompted him to choose *her* was a mystery. She must have been quite different back then.

*

The train sped smoothly toward Siena. Budding trees covered the landscape. It had rained the night before but now a wan sun was emerging and Maggie felt renewed. She would put on a better face, salvage the time they had left. They were in the country, away from the cars and crowds, and they still had five whole days.

Their hotel, a pretty brick building surrounded by flowers and trees, was on the outskirts of town, and the window of their room perfectly framed the city. The view was so nice, Maggie said, why didn't they forego a restaurant tonight and eat in the room; there was a small table they could pull under the window.

"This is more like it," said Maggie as they walked through the peaceful stone streets, passing tidy shops filled with cheeses and meats, colorful rows of produce. With every turn another vista opened up: age-old turrets, distant green hills. But the best sight, the real treat, was the sunlit expanse of a giant plaza that appeared suddenly before them. "The *Piazza del Campo*," said Ben, spreading his arms.

They had to stay. They had to sit in this wonderful, ancient marketplace and have a glass of wine. Ben said they should probably eat something to tide them over, and so they ordered an antipasto plate. Lounging in her chair, lazy with wine and sun, Maggie felt a tug of happiness, a second or two of perfect splendor, as if youth, carried on a breeze, had briefly, tenderly, touched her.

"These are my favorite," Maggie said, piercing a wrinkled black olive with a tiny wooden sword. "Aren't these great?" she said, raising the olive pick. "If I could just find a distributor."

Ben was looking out over the *piazza*. "You still have the price tag on those sunglasses," she told him. "It's stuck to the frame."

He pulled them off his face and removed the sticker. Putting them back on, he said, "This trip would have been hard on Helen, don't you think?" He turned to her; she could see her reflection in his sunglasses.

Maggie turned away from him and looked out over the plaza. "Yes. She would have had to miss a lot." She thought of their first day in Florence, that long climb up the Bell Tower.

A few days after Helen's accident, Ben had looked up from his dinner and said, suddenly, "You blame me. Don't you?" Maggie had been so shocked by the question, coming out of nowhere, that she couldn't speak right away, and Ben rushed out of the house. He was gone for hours. When he returned he went straight to the study, shutting the door behind him. Maggie stood motionless in the hallway; finally, through the door, she answered him: "I don't, Ben. I don't blame you." And this was true. No doubt she had wronged him in other ways, but this was a thought she would not allow. There was no reply.

*

On the way back to the hotel they stopped at a market and bought a wedge of gorgonzola, some fennel salami, a flat loaf of herb bread, two pears and a bottle of red wine. It was just as she imagined: They sat at the window, tree limbs in the foreground, Siena in the distance, a deeper gold each moment; and everything was superb, every bite, every sip.

Even so, Ben was distracted, oddly quiet, and Maggie found herself thinking about the night before, their last night in Florence, the awful dinner, the failed lovemaking, and gazing out at Siena, another beautiful city she would never grasp, Maggie wondered if travel wasn't better suited to the young, who didn't expect too much of a place, who moved through the world with ease and forgiveness. She almost expressed these feelings to Ben, and then thought better of it.

When the wine was three-quarters gone, when the gorgonzola was starting to ooze, to turn into something they no longer wanted, Ben said how about a little television; maybe they'd find something in English. And they did, only it was the news, and after listening to it for ten minutes they found they didn't care to know what was happening in America. They settled instead on a movie, "What's Eating Gilbert Grape." Because she had seen it, Maggie didn't mind the Italian dialogue, and soon she was wrapped up in the story, the sad, sad story of the obese mother and the children who adored her. At some point she started sobbing and couldn't stop, and she didn't know if it was the movie or the fact that they were reduced to watching it. At last Ben made her turn it off. They picked up the debris from dinner and pushed the table back where it belonged.

"Go wash your face," Ben said, rubbing her shoulders, "and

we'll walk into town."

It was getting dark, and as they walked through the stone streets they saw lights coming on, illuminating doorways, bringing signs and carvings to life.

"Are you chilly?" Ben said, bringing his arm around her shoulders.

"No," she replied, "but your arm feels nice."

Inevitably they were drawn into the plaza. Now it was a different world, softly lit, closer to antiquity. They stopped for a moment and looked up at the notched medieval rooftops, the single soaring tower.

"It's even prettier now," Ben said. He turned to her. "How about an espresso? We'll get a table somewhere."

No one wanted to serve them just coffee; if they wanted to sit down they had to order food.

"For Christ's sake," Ben said when they'd been turned away a third time. "It's not like they don't have room." And abruptly he stopped. "It's greed," he muttered. "Goddamn greed."

Maggie's stomach lurched. Ben almost never swore. She looked at his hunched shoulders, the defeat on his face. This was her doing.

She took his hand. "Come on, let's just walk for a bit." Gently she began leading him across the plaza.

"The moon's coming up," she said, pointing. A bright crescent, it hung beside the tower. "How many centuries have people stood here and looked at the moon?"

"Almost seven," Ben offered.

Reaching a narrow, sloping street, they paused. Darkness was total now and in the black crevices between the buildings, in the places they couldn't see, echoes were spilling into the night. A city this old, how could it contain all its secrets?

"Let's keep walking," Maggie said. "Let's pretend it's seven hundred years ago." They headed down the winding street, lit here and there with glowing lamps. "Imagine the people who've lived here," she whispered. It was a calming thought, all those lives that came before, lives no less full than her own. She ran her fingers down the cold pitted stone of a window sill. She studied the archways and heavy wooden doors, the elaborate pulls. Stopping at one shaped like a dragon, she reached out and grasped its smooth iron belly, then looked at her husband and smiled.

They were getting closer, she could feel it.

The Songbird Clinic

"Like this." Leslie touches the yellow beak of a baby bird and immediately the beak opens. Dropping in a bit of mush with a pair of plastic forceps, she says, "Don't worry about choking. The glottis closes to protect the lungs."

The bird, a robin, is only a few days old, nothing but a scrawny gray lump with a gaping beak. The raw need appalls me.

I recall something I read once about baby animals. Young reptiles are self-sufficient. They come into the world as tiny replicas of their parents and are quickly on their way. Baby mammals are helpless. To ensure they get the care they need, they are born cute, irresistibly so. But what about baby birds, helpless and ugly at once? I look at the knob of its head, the bulging eyes, still closed. What compels a mother bird to raise this frightful thing?

Like the other chicks at Cedar Bluff Bird Rescue, this tiny bird is an orphan: incidental damage. Maybe its nest blew down, or other birds drove the parents away, or the mother succumbed to a predator, most likely a house cat. That's what brought me here. My aging gray tabby killed a dove, the only bird slow enough for this rare event, which made me feel awful, and so I came here the next day and made a donation. One hundred dollars seemed like reasonable compensation for what my cat had done, though it felt odd to think of it that way. The last time I was in a pet store (I can't go into them anymore), I walked up to a cage of parakeets and peered at their blunt heads, their bodies colored like Easter eggs. They were on sale that day, $12 apiece, two for $20. For the cost of a movie and popcorn, you could buy a life, an exotic one at that. Your own little fraction of Australia to enjoy for years to come. Twelve bucks.

"You'll know when they've had enough," Leslie explains, "though there's bound to be one or two gluttons in the bunch." The volunteers, mostly older women, laugh. They listen closely to everything Leslie says, not wanting to make a mistake. They watch her hands, her posture, the way she moves. They barely breathe.

"If a chick won't feed, we probably can't save it. Sometimes they've had too much trauma. Chicks this young are always on the edge." She drops in another bit of mush. "Less than a third of baby birds survives their first year—most are lost in the first few weeks."

We absorb this information, our faces serious. Someone asks what sort of food Leslie is feeding the chick. "Mostly kitten chow," she says, "soaked in water, and we add a little hard-boiled egg and chopped-up mealworms. At this age, you'll be feeding them every twenty minutes, dawn to dusk—which is why we need all of you."

Leslie is a strapping woman, around 50, I'd guess. She has a thick silver braid down her back, a squared-off jaw and a hair-trigger smile. Her glasses have green frames and sit halfway down her nose. Her hands are large, her nails short. So far, I like everything about her.

When she took my check last week, she thanked me and then pointed to the Baby Songbird Clinic sign. "Orientation is this Saturday. We need all the hands we can get." She beamed at me. The smile was impersonal, involuntary, a wide-open welcome to the world. Doing right by this woman was the only way to go.

*

I signed up for the last shift, five-thirty to eight-thirty, three nights a week. Leslie was glad I took that time slot as most people want to be home in the evening. It makes no difference to me whether or not I'm home then, particularly now that I'm living alone. Right after Christmas, Jane moved out. I had changed, she said, and the gap between us was widening. "We've been together six years," I said. "Of course I've changed. You haven't?" She pursed her lips at this and looked out the window. You can't argue your way back into someone's heart, and so I let her go without much more dialogue, assuming she had found someone else, which, it turned out, she hadn't. That stung. For a while I wondered just what it was about the new me that Jane could no longer abide, and then I stopped because I didn't care enough, which of course proved her point. I wound up admiring her gumption.

My day job is not taxing: I purchase specialty foods for a high-end market, Babo and Tabani. Perfumed, well-coifed reps come to my office with their rolling cases of pomegranate honey and smoky onion mustard, and I decide which products land on the shelves. Once a year I go to a vast food show in Atlanta and wind my way through a sea of displays, stopping, tasting, moving on. Nothing prepared me for this vocation; anyone can do it, and don't think I'm unaware of the luck involved in sampling over-priced condiments for a living.

At the end of these breezy days, a few hours caring for baby birds is not too much to ask, and the clinic ends in mid-August. I do the feeding when I get there, and after that I make more formula, or smooth down the tips of the forceps, or line plastic nests with paper towels. The sides of these baskets are sloped as in nature, enough to keep the chicks safe, but not so steep that the birds can't defecate over the sides. This impresses me: baby birds, blind as bats, knowing to lift their tails so the nest stays clean.

In another part of this facility are the bigger birds: owls hit by cars, crows shot from the sky, vultures sick from lead ammo. I won't go into those rooms. I can't.

*

Megan, my younger sister, is a lawyer. And a marathon runner. And a violinist. And a sculptor. I wouldn't be surprised to hear that she has learned Mandarin, or taken up fencing, or invented a novel way to clean up marine oil spills. She usually pauses before she speaks and what comes out of her mouth is flawless and considered. People pay attention to Megan. She's smart alright, but what impresses me even more is her quiet avidity. She is like a leopard resting in a tree, still and keen at once.

Megan and I are on the phone, talking about the songbird clinic and the efforts involved in raising orphaned chicks. I picture her on her sofa, her slim legs curled beneath her, her lambent gaze focused on some elegant object in the room.

"I don't know how the parents do it," I say, "how they find all the bugs they need. And here we are dousing our yards with pesticides." This last distressing thought has not occurred to me till now.

"There doesn't seem to be as many hummingbirds this year," Megan says. "At least not here." Megan lives in a spacious home near Seattle, along with her husband Lyle and their two Great Danes. "You know, I don't recall any songbird clinics when we were kids. I guess we've lost the luxury of letting nature take its course."

"Yep. It's all mop-up now."

"The condors are coming back," she offers. This is a habit of hers, setting a bit of hope in front of me. "I just saw a program on them. There were once 22 left, but the latest count is around 400." In my fashion, I ignore the latter number and focus on the first, wondering if the condors knew it too, if their scarcity alarmed them. I picture this last group, huddled on the edge of oblivion, and I am sick to my stomach.

"Callie, it's wonderful what you're doing," Megan says. "Do you like it? Are you sublimating your maternal urges?" I can see her smiling.

I reflect on this. "It does make me think about how much power I have." I summon the rows of plastic nests, the birds lurching inside them, the frantic way they depend on what can't even see. "Here is this creature, smaller than a lemon, but it's a whole life. It's got the same force"—I grope for a comparison—"as a blue whale."

"Do you save most of them?"

"Yes—if they're strong enough to begin with." I consider the birds the volunteers never see, the ones that come in sick or hurt, the decisions that Leslie must make each day.

"You'd love Leslie," I say. "She's the program director. She's got this big booming laugh, and she's always telling people how well they're doing even when they're not." I offer an example of this, a nervous girl with shaky hands and the way Leslie calmed her, and then I describe Leslie's looks, her long braid and green glasses and easy stride, and Megan says:

"Sounds like you're sweet on her."

This brings me to a stop. Am I? Wouldn't I know this? Do 41-year-olds have crushes?

"I don't think so. I admire her, that's all."

"Oh no," says Megan. "The dogs are after something in the backyard. I gotta go."

"Okay. Call me next week."

"Will do."

I set my cell phone on the counter and summon up Leslie's image, waiting for a clue, a subtle, telling thrill. Can you lose the knack for love? A few days after Jane left, Megan reminded me that being alone had its compensations, that now I could fall in love all over again and what could be nicer than that? The thing is, these last four months haven't been terrible; they've been... restful: no need to make conversation, no worries about disappointing someone, no obligation to agree on menus or movies or dental products. If I do wind up falling in love again, I hope I'm up for it.

*

This morning I was having coffee on the deck when I noticed a spider web, about the width of a grapefruit, strung up between two of my potted vegetable plants. Three minute strands stretched from both sides, anchoring a tightly rigged web of breathless perfection, each miniscule partition exactly the same. Sitting in the middle of this web was an auburn spider the size of a pea. If the light had come from a slightly different angle, if I had not been looking that way at that instant, I would have missed him altogether and my world would be unchanged.

Nothing had flown into his perfect web, at least not recently, and I wondered if he was hungry and how long he went between meals, and if every web he made was this exquisite, and if they were all productive or if some webs proved worthless, and if a spider could become disheartened. A tiny movement on the periphery turned my attention to another bug, a green beetle with black stripes crawling out of a yellow cucumber flower. Knowing these beetles are trouble, I plucked it from the plant and held it between my thumb and forefinger, regarding the waving twin hairs of its antennae and the tiny hooked feet. It was nearly the size of the spider, and I thought what a feast it would be. I looked from one to the other. Here was the problem, here the solution. I could help a beneficial species and practice organic pest control at the same time.

Still, I had to get up the nerve to toss the beetle at the web; I was half hoping it would bounce off. It didn't. It stuck fast. In a blink, the spider shot down the web, seized the poor thing and stilled it just like that. Expertly, rapidly, the spider then began wrapping the carcass, enfolding it in sticky strands. In less than ten seconds, the beetle was a white mummy, and the spider, more leisurely this time, returned to the center of its web.

I've crushed more than a few troublesome bugs under my shoe, and I'm not sure why this death was so disturbing. Maybe because I trespassed, bullied my way into a place not designed for me, used another innocent creature to do my dirty work. How can I apologize? God was the only witness.

*

A lot of people think that only some birds, like ducks, bond with their caretakers. Wrong. Birds that can walk from birth are most susceptible, but all birds—all animals, in fact—imprint. Basically, they decide what they are during the first few weeks of their life; whoever feeds them is what they think they are. Because of this, we're not supposed to hold the chicks or have any contact with them beyond feeding; we're not even supposed to look at them too long, or from above, if we can help it—baby birds have predator fear and they don't like being peered down at. We're also cautioned not to talk loudly or use our cell phones. Another factor is heat. We use heating pads under the chicks without feathers, but the room is still kept very warm—a challenge for some of the menopausal volunteers.

So many things can go wrong with baby birds. Beyond drought, storms, predators and chemicals, there are hazards you'd never guess. Everything has to be just so, even the bottom of their nests—too smooth and the chicks' legs and feet don't get enough support. They wind up with something called "spraddle leg." People who try to raise chicks at home don't know this. They bring us these birds that can't walk right (Leslie calls them "swimmers") and want to know why. Also, people forget about giving the birds branches to perch on, or they give the birds branches that are too narrow or too wide, and the birds don't learn how to grip.

Lots of times the parent birds will discard their sick babies, nudge them right out of the nest—not a pleasant image, but that's how nature works: no looking back. People find these luckless chicks and bring them to us as if something can be done for them. People also bring in perfectly healthy birds, fledglings learning to fly. That's the mistake we see most often, and it's a shame because many of these birds die of stress, cornered in a shoebox, on their way to a rescue they never needed, while their parents are trying to find them.

*

I live in Napa Valley, which is not as romantic as it sounds, given the clogs of tourists, the sulfur spraying and the pre-dawn roar of the wind machines, but the beauty is a fair trade, and I'm not complaining. The vineyards turn lovely colors in autumn, and the clouds above them add to the splendor, especially when hawks are riding the thermals. Vultures like it here, too. On winter mornings you can see them lined up on the fence posts, six or seven in a row, spreading their enormous wings to the sun, ground fog rising around them.

From the deck of my apartment, I can see both sides of this valley, the green mountains to the west and the pink rocky hills to the east. There's some reassurance in this. I can't imagine living on the Great Plains, infinity on every side. All that time you have to watch a storm barreling down, knowing there's no escape.

I pay more for this apartment than it's worth (another drawback to living in this valley), and without Jane's income I have to be careful—not that I've ever been extravagant. I drive an ancient Honda Civic, and I hardly ever travel. Whatever clothes I need for work, I buy at discount stores. I got rid of the flat-screen TV after Jane moved out because the 300 channels were not worth the cost of the cable. I do have a cell phone and a computer, both outdated, but I'm not going to upgrade till I'm forced to. What I would like is more money for animal charities, which is something Jane and I had started to argue about and one more reason I don't mind living alone.

*

Another thing I didn't realize about baby birds is that they are born knowing how to fly. They don't need encouragement; they just need room. As soon as they have all their feathers and are eating on their own, we take them to the flight areas. There are three vinyl-screened aviaries at Cedar Bluff, and the young birds flutter around in them, trying out their wings and competing for food. In about two weeks they're ready for the world. Some we release right here; others are let go in areas that need re-populating.

I've seen Leslie free some of these birds, and she's just like a kid—all whoops and smiles, waving madly as they take to the sky. "Go be great," she yells, or, "Have a good life!" Watching her, you can't help smiling—at least I can't. That expression, to "get a kick" out of someone?—that's Leslie to a T. Her wholehearted laugh, her mismatched clothes, the flyaway hair around her face, the way she sometimes reaches out and squeezes my arm when she's talking to me. I haven't seen anything about her that isn't rock-bottom real.

Turns out she lives close to where I work. She says she walks over there now and then, that she adores the cheeses, and she told me I must be quite the gourmet, buying all that fancy food. I told her I wasn't, that as far as condiments go, looks matter more than flavor, and people will buy anything with a cheeky name and a little raffia. She laughed, but it's the truth. God help me if I ever start taking my job seriously.

*

In the mail this afternoon was a card from Megan, a photo of an old woman on a park bench feeding pigeons. The message read: "All that matters is what we do for each other." Inside the card was a check to Cedar Bluff Bird Rescue for $500. I looked at the check, smiling, loving my sister for the way she writes. Her handwriting, like everything else about her, is small and precise. I picked up my phone.

"Hello?"

"When I grow up," I said, "I want to be just like you."

"Not now you don't," Megan said. "One of the dogs just threw up in Lyle's office. Guess who's cleaning it up?"

"Yuck. Those dogs keep you running, don't they? I hope they're worth it."

"Oh they are. Absolutely."

"Should I call back?"

"No need. I just finished. Time for some wine." I can hear her heels clicking across the kitchen floor. "So, why do you want to be like me?"

"I got your card today. Wow, Megan. That's going to feed a lot of beaks."

"Good. And you'll be happy to hear I bought a bird feeder, too.

And a bluebird house. You see the power you have? I'll probably turn into one of those rabid bird watchers. Camo jacket. Ugly hat."

I laugh at this image. "You might."

"How's it going at Cedar Bluff?"

"We're starting to wind down. But I've been putting in a lot of hours, covering for other people."

"How much longer does it last?"

"Another couple of weeks. But there are things you can do after that—maintenance, fundraising, computer stuff. I might help out this winter."

"Interesting," Megan says, her tone teasing. "This wouldn't have anything to do with Leslie, would it?"

I say no, telling her that it's all about the birds, and it is; I want to help. But I did notice something last night when I was getting dressed to go to the clinic: I tried out three shirts in the mirror before I picked one. Beyond things like checking my teeth for food, I don't spend much time in front of mirrors, especially since Jane left. I think I need to be better about that, maybe spend a few minutes each day primping. Like my sister: Megan would never let her appearance lapse. I don't want to wind up like some wild-haired hermit, which is a risk you run when no one's looking.

*

Not all baby birds can eat kitten chow. People bring us pigeons, too, and they eat what their parents regurgitate. We feed them a special formula, using syringes, and we have to do this slowly and make sure we don't overfill their crops. And because the formula hardens like cement, we have to be careful about washing off their beaks and necks afterward. The trade-off is they don't need to be fed nearly as often as the other birds. I think I like the doves and pigeons best of all, the good-natured way they meander around. And their cooing. Such soft, bubbling notes, as if they arise from a musical instrument, as if these birds were put here to calm us.

I worry a lot about the pigeons and doves we release—they spend so much time on the ground, and they don't move quickly. We need to make sure they're eating well and that they're preening, which we encourage by misting them with water. After we've done all we can, we take these faultless creatures to a park and hope the world makes room for them.

*

Megan may be right. When Leslie asked me this afternoon if I wanted to come by her place sometime, I felt my neck get warm.

"Sure," I said. "When?"

She grinned, shrugged. "How about tonight? I've got some of that wicked cheese you sell, and some wine." She pulled a container of bird food out of the microwave and tested it with her finger. "You can follow me from here if you want."

"Great," I said, beaming at the pin-feathered robin in front of me.

*

Leslie lives in a cottage in her landlord's backyard. It is a wooden structure half-covered in vines, and when you look at the arched door and the wavy glass in the windows, you expect to find elves inside. On the porch is a collection of pots from which various plants rise and droop, and over the doorway is a plaque decorated with a line of crows and these words: Primitive Gatherings.

Leslie pauses, her hand on the doorknob, and looks at me over her shoulder. "You don't mind dogs, right?"

"I love dogs," I assure her, which I do.

"These two won't attack. They might not even get up."

She pushes open the door, snaps on a light and we walk into a cozy living area that holds a maroon velvet sofa, a burl wood coffee table, a bookcase and two dog beds. On the far end of the sofa is an end table and a lamp with an amber mica shade. The room is cool and smells like deep woods. One of the dogs, a stiff-legged Jack Russell, rises from his bed and hobbles over on his three legs. "That's Kevin," says Leslie. "He needs to smell you." Kevin eyes me carefully, then sniffs my feet and ankles. In a moment, the stub of his tail starts to wag. "You pass!" she says.

"And that's Molly." The other dog, a brown Chihuahua, studies me warily from her bed. "She's okay, a little more nervous than Kevin. They're both rescue dogs."

"How old are they?"

Leslie leans close and whispers. "Old. They don't like me to mention their ages." She turns, beckons me with one hand. "Follow me. You can pour the wine."

We walk into a tiny kitchen brimming with food: potatoes suspended in wire baskets, bananas browning in a big chipped bowl, dried herbs dangling from the rafters, grains sitting in glass jars. The countertop is a great slab of wood; the white sink, big enough to wash a collie, is old and streaked with rust. I think of my own kitchen, everything tucked away, the glossy granite counters, the stainless steel sink, no sign of food anywhere.

"It's kind of messy right now," Leslie says, pulling packages of cheese from the fridge. She stops, looks at me, lets out a laugh. "Hell, it's always messy!"

"I love it," I say, almost fiercely. I do. I wish I lived in a place like this. I look at the window over the sink, the plants rooting in tiny jars. I want plants like that on my windowsill.

"There's some Merlot over there," she says, nodding toward a shelf to my left. "And I have a white here if you'd rather have that. Pinot Grigio."

"Yes," I say, "the white." Leslie opens a cupboard, takes out two wine glasses and hands them to me. "I'll have the Merlot," she tells me.

I pour the wine, and she unwraps some packages of cheese and sets them on a plate, along with a fistful of seeded crackers. "I live on cheese," Leslie says. She pats her hip and grins. "Can you tell?"

We move into the living room and Leslie sets the cheese tray on the coffee table.

"Have a seat," she says. "Not much choice here, I'm afraid. But I like it. It's quiet, and my landlord's a dream."

I settle onto one end of the sofa and Leslie drops down on the other. Kevin is back in his bed, but Molly comes over quietly and lies on the braided rug, resting her chin on Leslie's foot. On the wall in front of us are two photographs, both of young men, one laughing and waving from a canoe, the other looking up from a book.

"My boys," she says, and points to them. "Danny and Joel."

Danny is blonde and broad shouldered; Joel has dark hair and a solemn look. Of course Leslie would have children. I never wanted children, not for a minute, and I'm surprised at the number of women who do, who relinquish themselves so easily.

"Danny looks like you," I say.

"He does. And Joel looks just like this father. Ted." She reaches for her wine. "We're divorced. Good friends, though."

"How long have you lived here?"

"Four years. Since I got back from Costa Rica. I was there for nine years."

"Nine years! What were you doing in Costa Rica?"

"Ted and I heard about this animal sanctuary there, so we went down to help. It's a spider monkey rehab." Leslie reaches for a cracker and smears it with a soft cheese. "After a couple or years, he started missing the States, so he moved back, and I stayed on."

I look at her a moment with quiet amazement. "What was it like, taking care of spider monkeys?"

She takes off her glasses and rubs her eyes. "It's hard stuff, Callie. I've rescued all kinds of animals, but primates are different." She pauses and looks at me. "They're like us, their sounds, their movements, their needs. The first one you hold, you see that. It knocks the wind out of you."

"Why do they need rescue?"

She frowns. "The power lines, mainly. They're being strung up everywhere, and of course the spider monkeys think they're vines. Sometimes just the mother gets killed, or injured, and sometimes the baby too, at the same time. It's awful."

I tear up at this and for a moment I can't talk. I look down at the rug. "I don't know how you did it," I murmur, "how you could see that every day for nine years."

Leslie shrugs. "It's more than wound care. You have to discipline them. Sometimes you have to leave them alone so they won't attach, so they can be freed, and they don't like that. They don't want to let go of you." She leans forward and puts her hands on her knees. "We did manage to release quite a few of them."

I lift my palms in a gesture of helplessness. "They're still putting up power lines, right? Did you give up? Is that why you came back?"

Leslie stares at me a moment. It's an expression of regret, one I've never seen on her. "I got tired, Callie. I didn't give up. I never thought that what I did didn't matter. The monkey you're holding— that's the one that matters. Just like the songbirds."

I shake my head, loathing myself. "I could never do what you did. The birds are hard enough."

Leslie regards me, her expression softening. "Lots of people can't, Callie. They come to monkey rehabs and leave a few days later. But when they get home, they start writing checks, and we need that as much as we need caregivers—more even. Do you think Cedar Bluff would be there without the donations we get?"

This makes me feel a little better, and I offer a slight smile. She reaches across the sofa and pats my thigh.

"Takes all kinds, kiddo," she says. "But enough of that." She picks up her wine, leans forward and clicks her glass against mine. "Cheers."

We look at each other, a look you can't name or pin any hopes on, a look I've shared with a thousand people, on the street, in a store. A connection is all it is, the briefest acknowledgment that this is common ground.

Salvage

I am 99 years old. I do not expect to see 100, nor is it a goal of mine. Others have begun to show interest, to root for me (for all I know they are placing bets), but I don't give a damn about that milestone. What is a number compared to a life?

Some want to know the secrets to my longevity, what I eat and drink, if I consider myself an optimist, that sort of thing. Anyone who has lived as long as I have will tell you the same thing: There are no secrets, you are on your own. I suppose you might better the odds with exercise and the right food; I never tried. People born before 1900 ate and drank what was there; none of us knew a thing about preservatives or saturated fats or high fructose corn syrup until long after we'd consumed quantities of them. Don't lecture me about the dangers of red dye #4. I drink Manhattans—yes, still—and can't tell you how many maraschino cherries I've sent down the hatch.

My arteries, along with everything else, have stiffened up. They tell me I have heart disease, as if that's news. They say I could go at any time—again, not news. "Maybe in your sleep," the cardiologist said last week, giving my hand a reassuring pat. This does not comfort me, the idea of falling asleep and never waking. I want to be there, to see it, to feel it. I can't believe that anyone dies without knowing. I think there must be a little tap on the shoulder, a few seconds of clarity before the next world bears us away. Even if there is nothing after, even if I go out like an old television screen, a vanishing white dot and then a gray blank, I have a hunch that those last few seconds will be worth the cost.

I can't drive anymore and my hearing isn't good, but my mind is still spry, if wayward. It's true what they say about memories of youth becoming more vivid with age. Though I often forget where I left my book or glasses, I can draw you a map of the flour mill I worked in when I was a girl. I can hear those stone grinders moving, can smell the buckwheat being crushed into meal, can see the powder on my skirt. There is John, grinning at me, his face coated white; there he is, pulling me close, kissing me behind a bin of corn. These stories keep coming to me, as if my mind, bored with current conditions, sneaks away, plays hooky with the past. That was you, it reminds me, you had that, you did that. Claim tickets, that's what memories amount to. A friend of mine has Alzheimer's; she doesn't know me, she doesn't know anyone. I can't imagine that endless fog, being lost inside your own life.

My great granddaughter, Liza, attends college in Eugene and is majoring in journalism. She is on her summer break and has been coming by to "interview" me. I love this girl. Liza has no guile, not a smidge. She expects to find the good in you, and so she does. Innocence must be a gene, a recessive one, because only a few folks are born with it. I hope she stays this way, that her goodness is a match for this world.

Liza is not asking me questions about my diet. What she wants to know is how I lived, what Oregon was like in 1895, the year I was born. She is thrilled by my descriptions of the hats and corsets we wore, the horse-drawn buggies we relied on. She never tires of hearing about the drafty house I grew up in, alongside my three brothers, one who perished at the age of 5, as so many children did back then. We had no central heating, no indoor plumbing, no phone, no car (there weren't any cars to be had west of the Mississippi River). My brothers went to work instead of high school. I got through school alright, but most of my education came much later, by way of night classes and the public library. My father made $3000 a year repairing farm equipment; we saw him only at dinner. My mother died at age 45, three years sooner than average.

Liza is collecting this information for an essay she hopes to publish. She has asked for my permission and I've given it.

Today I will tell her about my husband John and my son Frankie. Like the rest of the family, she knows only the bare facts. I never wanted to talk about the Santa Clara and people knew this, left me alone with it. Now I am ready to tell the story, partly because it seems mingy not to, like taking a recipe to your grave. And what if I am the last person on earth who lived through that night? People should know what happened to us; there should be a record, something to lay hands on, something not lost to the waves.

*

We were living in Salem then, with John's folks. I was 20, John was 24. He was working for his father, in the flour mill, and I was helping out there, too. He didn't like the mill. He wanted to see San Francisco, where his brother lived. Henry had a job building ships. He told John it was good paying work and you didn't have to be cooped up all day. John wanted to visit Henry and those shipyards. I was nervous about traveling with the baby, but John wanted to go so badly.

It wasn't like people think. You mention ship travel and they think Titanic—private baths, telephones, fancy staircases, ladies in long white gloves. Those old steam schooners were nothing like that. All you had was a bunk in the wall, two or three in each room, and there was a little sink, and that green can near the head of your bunk—you knew what *that* was for pretty quick. Only one of you could stand at a time, that was all the room there was.

Whatever you brought, they put below. You slept in your clothes—if you could sleep. Everybody got seasick. The smell was terrible. They had this mechanical piano in the dining room, to try and make things cheerful, I guess, but no one put any money in it. The food wasn't too bad—of course we didn't feel much like eating.

There was a nice woman traveling with her little boy. He must have been 7 or so, sweet little thing, had a limp from polio. His mother and I talked for quite a while. Her husband was in San Francisco, waiting for them.

There were four children, including Frankie. He was the only baby, though—13 months. Looked just like his father. Dark blue eyes, wavy hair. He'd just started walking.

We all went to our rooms after lunch. No one wanted to be up on deck. It was cold, the wind had picked up. Nothing to look at anyway, just gray sky, gray waves. John and I got in our bunks. We hadn't slept much the night before and we were tired, but it was no use trying to sleep, not with the ship tossing like it was, and Frankie fussing. There was nothing for him to do, no place to play.

It was late afternoon when we hit that reef. Oh my, what a jolt. I was lying with my back to the wall, holding the baby, but John was sitting on the edge of his bunk and he got knocked to the floor. He jumped right up, wide-eyed, told me to stay put, that he'd find out what was going on.

It got my attention alright, but I wasn't in a panic. I knew we had life boats and life vests, if we needed them. I'd never been on a ship. I trusted the crew, I guess, figured they knew what they were doing.

John came back a few minutes later. He said we were close to shore and that everything would be fine. I could hear people talking outside the room. Everyone was in the hall, all talking at once.

The captain rang the bell then, four times—we all knew that was the distress call, and everybody started rushing for the deck. The children were crying, a few of the women, too.

The ship started to turn then, slowly, you could feel the pulling under your feet. It was hard to walk, and we were tilted, we kept bumping into each other. And the *noise*—you wouldn't think a ship could groan like that. I remember feeling sorry for it—isn't that odd?

It was getting dark by then and raining hard, didn't take more than a couple minutes to get soaked through. Mind you, the clothes were heavier then, made from wool. All the women wore woolen stockings and those long treacherous skirts. Felt like you were lugging the world around once you got wet.

The ship turned two, maybe three times, and then it started leaning more, sending us all to one side. Someone said the bow had a hole in it and water was coming in. We could see the shore then, or at least the lights on it. Folks must have known we were in trouble and were getting ready to help.

The captain was there. Gus was his name. Poor man was trying to figure out what to do. One of the men said we should stay on the ship, that the sea was too rough, but the captain was afraid we'd sink—he had us start putting on life jackets, told the crew to lower the lifeboats.

You couldn't fault the crew. They were kind, helping us tie on the life jackets and get into the boats. They were trying real hard to keep folks calm, making sure things were kept orderly.

The wind was blowing and the rain was coming down hard on the deck, and everyone was shouting over the noise, but they finally got us loaded up. John was in the second boat, I was in the first, with the rest of the women and children.

There was no moon, just the dark sky and rain coming down. Nobody was talking, we were all just hanging onto the sides of the boat, looking toward the beach. One of the crewmen was rowing, having a hard time of it. A couple of us tried to help him, but we weren't much use.

I think we were about halfway to the beach when the boat turned sideways and a big comber hit us. Picked us right up out of the ocean like we were nothing and flipped us over.

I lost Frankie right away. The water was so cold, and that life vest—they were bulky back then, you couldn't get a proper hold on things.

I couldn't feel my legs, couldn't catch my breath. I kept reaching out, all around, trying to find Frankie, trying to keep my head above the waves. Behind me I heard people crying for help. They were hanging onto the overturned boat. I felt a hand on my arm and someone was pulling me over. I grabbed one of the boat ribs, hung on as tight as I could. I called and called for Frankie, but it was no use. The surf kept pounding the boat, smashing us against it. My legs were useless; my arms felt like they were being pulled out of their sockets. Some poor souls slipped off. I don't know how I kept my hold, but I finally felt the sand under me. People were pulling me onto the beach.

The second boat overturned too, someone said. I kept asking about John, but no one had seen him. There were all kinds of people trying to help, handing out blankets, giving us food and coffee. They said I needed to get to the hospital, but I wouldn't leave. They were shining lanterns on the people washed up, trying to find the survivors. When I saw two people carrying a man in a green coat, I knew it was John. I remember how his hands looked, hanging down, so long and white; I knew he was dead. They didn't find Frankie that night, not that there was any hope for him.

The hospital was full, so they took us to private homes, people with the room to take us in. I wound up in North Bend, with the Cabots. Alfred Cabot was a doctor. He bandaged me up, set my legs—my ribs were fractured and I'd broken both legs. I stayed there ten weeks, till I could walk again.

They found Frankie two days after the wreck. The Cabots didn't want me to see him, but I insisted, so they brought him to me. Course he didn't look like himself anymore. It was terrible. It was like being ripped in two. We had a service for him there in the room. They were good people, the Cabots. We stayed in touch for years.

The captain lived—he probably wished he hadn't. They found him negligent, took away his license. He was being punished, you see, for putting us into those lifeboats.

That ship would have held together for days, and it did. Looters started climbing aboard, taking whatever they could. They had it pretty much emptied in a few days, whatever hadn't been ruined by leaking oil or water. Someone finally set fire to it, just for the spectacle.

We never needed those lifeboats. We could have used the gangplank. The next day, at low tide, we could have walked to shore without even getting our feet wet.

The wreck of the Santa Clara. You can look it up. Coos Bay, November 2, 1915. 48 passengers, 42 crewmen, 14 dead—or assumed dead; not all the bodies came back. That's as much as you'll learn from the newspapers.

I wanted to die of course, could not understand why I hadn't, what point there was in sparing me when all I had left was pain. A life without John and Frankie did not seem possible, and all I could do while my bones stitched themselves together was think about Frankie, slipping from my arms, and John's ghostly hands.

You want to die, but you don't, you can't. Your life keeps towing you along. In that bed, half-mad with misery, I could not have conceived that five years later I would marry a watchmaker named Alan Collins, that I would lose him too when a piece of roofing slid from the hands of a carpenter and struck him on his way to work; or that two years after this, I would marry a third time, a banker named Clyde Odell, and promptly give him twins; that we would wind up in a big gabled home in Portland, which is now worth a fortune; that I would live to the age of 99. Maybe longer.

Breach

Amy pulled back the gauze and peered at the wound on her leg, a series of raised welts capped with dried blood. It looked worse today, she thought. Puffier. Maybe infection was setting in; these beautiful places were treacherous. Just last week she had read about a man who suffered a minor cut on his leg while zip lining in Jamaica and died eight days later. "Don't touch the coral," the instructor had warned, and she hadn't. Not with her hands.

She panicked, that's what happened. They'd all been given little bags of frozen peas, which they were told to dispense gradually, and it was fun at first to let loose a pea and watch the fish arrive in their hot bright colors. They flashed around her face and body, and then she felt them on her legs, bumping, nipping, she wasn't sure. Picturing all those urgent, rigid mouths on her flesh, she spilled the bag of peas, and suddenly there were fish everywhere, darting past her shoulders, shooting up from below. One, electric blue and as long as her arm, had an underbite loaded with spiny white teeth. She flailed in the water, tried to backpedal, her flippers pulling hard, and then her leg smacked the coral and she yelped into her snorkel. Two seconds later she thought of her blood, streaming into the ocean, and the opening scene in the movie Jaws, and that's when she broke the surface and screamed for Dinah.

Who just now came out of the bathroom, smiling and flushed, wearing nothing but a white towel. She walked over to the sliding glass doors and stood there, hands on her hips, admiring the view: palm trees, white sand, turquoise ocean—exactly as the brochure had promised. Amy regarded Dinah's strong shoulders and plump, muscled calves.

"This place rocks," she said, turning around. Her blonde hair fell in wet ringlets around her shoulders. Dinah was short and strong.

"Dinah-mo," their friends called her. She ran a catering business and often worked 18-hour days with no sign of fatigue. "I love that seat in the shower, don't you? So much easier shaving your legs."

This time, their third trip to Hawaii, they were staying at the Four Seasons in Wailea, in an oceanfront suite. Amy, who made good money at Benson Accountancy, opted at the last minute to splurge. While Dinah had not wanted to spend so much money on a room, she changed her mind the moment they walked in. "Oh my," she said, setting her purse on a marble-topped writing desk. She swept past the plush furniture and potted palms and stopped at the doors leading out to the lanai, beyond which glittered the blue Pacific; a mauve mountain floated in the distance. "We're ruined," she remarked. "I hope you know that."

"What do you want to do today?" Dinah asked. "How's your leg?"

"I'm not sure," Amy said. "I think it might be a little worse."

"Let me see." Dinah approached the chair Amy was sitting in, and once more Amy pulled back the bandage. Dinah looked at the scrape and frowned. "Looks about the same to me. Does it hurt?"

"Only if I bump it."

"Does it feel hot?"

Amy shook her head.

"Then don't worry about it. They got antibiotic on it as soon as you came out of the water. You're fine. But I guess you won't be doing any more snorkeling."

"I don't care—the water's too cold anyway. Didn't you get cold yesterday?"

"A little," Dinah admitted. She leaned in closer, kissed Amy's forehead. "Give me ten minutes, then we'll get some breakfast. I'm starving."

*

High above their heads palm fronds clattered in the breeze. Amy peered up, hypnotized by the metallic flashes of sun on the rippling leaves. Orange and yellow hibiscus flowers nodded from a hedge beside their table. A few feet away two zebra doves cooed at one another and bobbed their heads. Yesterday, in a cove not far from the resort, Amy and Dinah had spotted a group of turtles swimming in a sun-struck cavern. Over and over the creatures swam above and beneath each other in what appeared to be a gentle form of play. For over an hour, perched on a large black rock, Amy and Dinah had watched them, not wanting to break away from something so lovely and rare.

Amy forked up a piece of sausage and studied the larger dove that was now puffing out its striped breast.

"Have you noticed that everything here seems to be in love?" she said. "Birds, turtles—I think the palms are in love with the wind."

Dinah lifted a wedge of her Sunrise Quesadilla. "Who wouldn't love this place?"

"Funny how you can't live here, though. I mean, once you move here it isn't paradise."

Dinah frowned. "I don't know about that."

"It's true. That sales girl at Banana Republic yesterday? I chatted with her when you were trying on pants. She has three jobs and two roommates and she still can't afford to live here. She's moving back to the mainland as soon as she can scrape up the air fare."

Dinah chewed, considered. "Yeah. I guess it wouldn't be much fun being poor in paradise. Still you'd have all this." She spread an arm across the sweep of the ocean. "In the middle of January."

Amy nudged an orange slice of papaya to the edge of her plate. She was getting tired of papayas. And mangoes, and pineapples, and guavas, and passion fruit. Not that they weren't delicious, just that they were everywhere. There was a mountain of whole fruit in the middle of the buffet, and bowls and bowls of cut fruit scattered down the table. The bounty of these islands, the wanton, unstoppable life. Philodendrons three stories high. Orchids surging out of tree trunks.

Amy regarded a huge yellow hibiscus flower inches from her arm; it looked like it wanted something from her; she could almost hear it panting.

"Even if I had the money," Amy said, "I think I'd go crazy after a while—island fever. I'd start wanting things I couldn't have. Redwoods. Fall foliage. Fresh apples."

"San Francisco," Dinah added. They lived in Novato and drove into San Francisco at least once a month for dinner or plays or exhibits, sometimes just to walk through the Castro and see what the boys were up to.

Amy felt a tickling sensation in her wound and pictured a legion of bacteria assembling there, hoisting tiny vicious picks, ready to start work. It seemed she had already used up a large portion of her fear and now she was more curious than anything else. Wouldn't it be something, with this lump under her arm, to die of a scrape? That zip liner probably had no idea what was happening to him. She pictured him in some thatch-covered island bar, popping a few ibuprofen and eyeing the native girl who was bringing him drinks.

It might be nothing of course, the lump. It probably *was* nothing, Dr. Stark had said. But Amy had watched the doctor's face as her fingers explored the area, had seen the wary attentiveness. "When do you first notice this?" Dr. Stark asked.

Amy mustered a light tone. "A few months ago, I guess." The doctor tightened her lips and prodded the flesh around the lump.

"Has it grown?"

"I'm not sure. Not much, anyway." Amy could actually feel it now when she pressed her arm to her side.

"It doesn't move," the doctor said, dropping her hand. "Does it hurt?"

"No. Not at all." From the doctor's slight frown Amy understood that this was not the optimum answer. The doctor returned to her seat and typed something into the computer. "You're a little thin."

"I don't think I've lost any weight," Amy said.

The doctor gave a shrug. "Four pounds since your last exam. Any fatigue? Fever or chills?" she asked, keeping her eyes on the monitor.

"No."

Dr. Stark looked over at Amy. "It's probably just a cyst or a fatty growth, but we need to do some imaging and a biopsy. I want you to come in next week."

Amy swallowed hard. She was at a disadvantage here, in this paper vest, perched on a table, waiting for orders. She needed clothes, a proper chair. "I'm going to Hawaii on Monday. Can I come in the week after?"

The doctor nodded and turned back to the computer. "That's fine, but no later."

*

Amy and Dinah looked hard but could not see the turtles. The water was choppier today and they could barely make out the cavern. After a few moments, they climbed down from the rock and began walking along the beach. Great clouds hung over the ocean, which was vast and grey and ruffled with whitecaps. The wind was warm and constant.

"Look," said Dinah, pointing. Far out, the great black tail of a humpback broke from the sea. Seconds later, another, and then another. "Wow. Must be a whole pod."

Amy, thrilled, began counting. What was it about whales? Why did they cause such a stir? Their monstrous proportions, or the fearsome depths they rose from without warning?

"I've seen thirteen," she said. "They don't look real, do they? From here they look, I don't know, prehistoric."

"They do," said Dinah. "They look mythic."

After a while they turned back toward the hotel, and as they walked they discussed how they might spend the last three days of their vacation.

"Are we still getting tattoos on Friday?" Dinah asked. This had been the plan, to go to Lahaina the day before they left and get their first tattoos. Dinah had decided on a string of ivy around her ankle; Amy was considering something small—a bird or a turtle, maybe—on her shoulder.

Now, however, Amy was having second thoughts. It wasn't the pain that gave her pause—that, she'd heard, was minor; it was the idea of a permanent stain, of ink sinking into her pores and staying there. This was her skin, the tender wrapping she came in. Branding it felt willful. Like trespassing.

"I'm not sure," Amy said. "You can."

"Chickening out on me?" said Dinah, neatly skirting the foamy wash of a wave.

"Something like that." She did not want to share her misgivings and squelch Dinah's enthusiasm—not that she could. Dinah was an eager sort, always ready for a new adventure and not inclined to deliberate. The mishaps and rapid-fire alterations involved in catering were hurdles she was born for.

"Well, you've been wanting a new pendant—maybe you can shop for that while I'm in the tattoo place." Dinah moved closer and reached for Amy's hand. "What about today. What do you want to do? We could go zip lining. They have half-day tours."

Amy shuddered. "No thank you. Not after reading about that guy in Jamaica."

"Amy. Thousands of people zip line every day with no problem. That was a freak thing."

"Maybe." Amy looked out at a long red boat that was moving rapidly over the water. "I just don't see the attraction—hanging from a cable, zipping over the scenery. Shouldn't we be slowing down here, smelling the lotus?"

Dinah laughed. "What a cranky pants you are. I think we need to get you a Mai Tai." She let go of Amy's hand and ventured over to a dark still form on the sand.

"Oh god—it's a baby seal."

Amy approached the lifeless creature, which was black and about three feet in length; it had not been dead long. "It's a monk seal," she murmured. "They're endangered." She had read a lot about Hawaii, "the extinction capital of the world," and its lost species.

"I wonder what happened to it," said Dinah.

"Probably something happened to the mother. Normally they don't leave their newborns, not for weeks." Amy felt her throat thicken; she blinked back sudden tears. "Life is horrible," she said. "It really is. It's horrible."

"C'mon," said Dinah, taking gentle hold of Amy's arm.

"Wait," Amy snapped. She couldn't just walk away as if this animal had meant nothing. She squatted down and laid a hand on its cold wet fur. She looked at the closed eyes and the whiskers, and then she looked down the beach at the heartless palms, the string of hotels. Finally she got to her feet.

"We should tell someone."

*

They were driving up to Kapalua, where they had decided to spend the afternoon. The northwest coast was supposed to be great for whale watching, and not overrun with people. From a store near the their hotel, Amy and Dinah had purchased a bottle of wine, some soft cheese and a box of water crackers (they wanted a baguette but the market sold only local breads and these were all studded with banana or pineapple). The hotel sent them on their way with two enormous mangoes, which Amy accepted with a false show of delight.

The ocean, which had turned from grey to sapphire, rolled by on the left, each glorious vista surpassing the one before. Dinah, who was driving, looked over at Amy and said, "Remember the Road to Hana?"

Of course she did. Who didn't remember that road? Fun for the first couple miles, punishment for the next thirty. Like many couples, they had given up halfway—all those sickening turns through a jungle that grew increasingly ominous. And when they did stop to quell their nausea, the mosquitos were unbearable.

"This is so much nicer," Amy said, determined to be agreeable, to prize what pleasure she could from these last few days here. "Thanks for suggesting a picnic—I don't think there's anything I'd rather do more." Dinah, keeping her eyes on the road, smiled.

They had been together almost two decades, had unwittingly achieved such a durable base that separation was neither conceivable nor possible. They'd had problems of course, like any other couple, flare-ups that came with the territory: a cook living with an accountant. Early on, there were even agonizing affairs— simultaneous, one apiece—from which they'd eventually, amazingly, recovered. Trust could be broken, they'd learned, but just once....surely, just once. Maybe, Amy thought now, their relationship had never really been threatened, never been in danger at all. Was that possible in this world?

Amy shifted in her seat, pretended to study the scenery. Her hand stole beneath her shirt and moved up to her armpit. For a moment she fingered the lump, which did seem larger now. Last night, making love, she was nervous that Dinah would find it.

Amy had not told Dinah about the lump, not yet. There was no point in worrying them both. She would tell her later, when she knew more. This was the snag about love—no one was spared. For as long as possible she wanted Dinah to be free.

Which was another downside to having a partner—had she been single, Amy would have postponed this trip. Instead, not wanting to disappoint Dinah, she had upped the ante, had arranged for expensive accommodations, as if such defiance would surmount all else. It hadn't. Sometimes the fear took her breath away; mostly it worked as a filter through which everything showed its flaws. She shook her head, remembering last night, comparing it to the lovemaking of their first trip here, when there were no intrusive thoughts, when there was only hunger followed by pleasure, their ardor a tease, waiting to claim them at the end of each day.

Amy looked out her window at what appeared to be fields of sugar cane. There was even a sweetness in the air. They set fire to these fields before harvest, she'd read, to burn off the tops and leaves. She pictured the crackling flames, the clouds of grey smoke rising over the island. It seemed a violent solution.

She turned back to Dinah, who appeared, as usual, faintly contented, one hand on the wheel, her elbow resting on the open window. She had a temper, for sure, but it left as fast as it came; mostly she was fine with life. She was probably not thinking about burning fields right now.

"When we get back to the hotel," Amy said, "we can check out those zip line tours. Maybe we can go tomorrow."

Dinah looked over. "Really?"

"What the hell," said Amy, lifting a shoulder.

"Exactly!" Dinah grinned.

*

They parked on a ridge high above the ocean. Across the water, softy draped in blues and greens, was the island of Molokai. White clouds hung over its peaks and valleys. On the left side of the beach, a string of black rocks stretched into the sea. The sand itself was pink. Amy stood next to the car, lunch in hand, trying to take in the scene. She could not. This is what was meant by "impossible beauty." You absorbed what little you could, and then you gave up.

"It's kind of steep," said Dinah, who was eyeing the path to the beach. "But we can do it. We'll just go slow." She turned around. "Is your leg okay?"

"It's fine," Amy said, realizing that it was; she hadn't even thought of it since breakfast.

Crowded by the rampant plant growth, they side-stepped their way down to the beach, pausing at the bottom to smell the sea-drenched air and gaze again at the island set before them like a gift from a munificent god. Brilliant flashes of sun rippled over the water. As if instructed, they walked to the rocky arm of the beach and found a place near the cliff to spread their towels.

They drank some wine, watched two sanderlings dash back and forth through the lapping waves. Above them, a white tern sailed.

"I heard you get up last night," Dinah said. "What were you doing?"

Amy pressed her plastic cup into the sand. "I went out on the lanai." She smiled, remembering. "I took off my top."

"You did?"

"It was wonderful. Now I know why women in Tahiti go topless. Really. It's reason enough to move there." Amy recalled the dark palms fronds moving above her, the white crests on the ocean, the muffled roar of the waves. Half naked, arms open, she felt like she was offering herself, to the night, the wind. She tried to explain this now to Dinah: the warm wind on her breasts, how vulnerable she felt, but powerful, too, both of these at once.

"Wow," said Dinah. I'm definitely trying that tonight."

"Damnit," said Amy, who was looking over Dinah's shoulder. "Why do they keep showing up?"

"What?"

"Men."

Dinah turned and regarded the figure walking their way, a lone man wearing a large brimmed hat; a pair of binoculars hung around his neck. "He looks harmless enough," she said. "And you do have a shirt on right now."

A commotion at sea drew their attention. Two large animals—presumably whales—were thrashing in the water, rolling over and over each other, the ocean breaking around them. Amy and Dinah got to their feet. The man, who was close to them now, stopped and studied the animals through his binoculars.

"Are they fighting?" said Dinah, "or mating?"

"Neither," said the man, lowering his binoculars. "They're juveniles. They're playing."

No matter where you went on vacation, Amy thought, there was always a slight man in Dockers and a sunhat who knew everything there was to know about whatever spectacle you were looking at. Not that she wasn't grateful for the information—teenagers frolicking!

"Lots of whales out there today," he added, and not five seconds later, a little farther out, the great fan of a humpback's tail came suddenly into view.

"They're breeding now, aren't they?" Amy asked.

The man nodded. "That's what they come down here for, breeding and birthing. The calves do better in warmer waters."

A woman with two children walked up. They stopped a few feet from where the man stood. "Hello," the woman said, smiling. "Aren't they wonderful?"

Now they were a crowd, as it seemed they should be with something like this in front of them. Amy looked back at the rolling pair, who were making quite a racket smacking the water.

And then, off to the right, an enormous whale surged out of the sea, all the way, the ocean pouring off its body, its great fins and belly white against the blue sky. In the instant that it hung in their world, this magnificent, improbable beast, Amy threw her arms up and whooped, as they all did—they could not help themselves, as if whatever ecstasy that sent this creature out of sea had rushed into them, and when the whale fell back, in a tremendous splash, they felt in their own bodies the sound of its weight.

Afterward they all beamed at one another, helplessly, and then they began to speak, sharing their joy. Wasn't that the most amazing thing they had ever seen? Was it their first time? What did it mean when whales breached? Even the man in the hat did not know the answer to that one.

Dinah, who had at some point caught hold of Amy's hand, hugged her now and said, "That was worth the price of the trip."

Amy looked back at the ocean, at the place where this marvel had occurred. It must have felt wonderful, that instant of dominion, that pause between the rising and the falling. There was no other way to account for the effort.

Parasites

Julie had gotten out of the car to pee, Marc said, and the next thing he knew she was gone. Over the edge. He never heard a thing.

That was the story Marc gave the police. Nora thought this was a clever embellishment, this addition of a bodily function. Did he come up with it before or after? He must have smiled when the idea arrived. His cold heart must have fluttered.

Did he push her? What better way to kill someone and get away with it? Plan a trip to the Grand Canyon, or the Dover cliffs, or the Mayan ruins—this world abounds with fatal attractions—then pick your moment. You could pretend to take a picture before barreling down; or you just stand there shoulder to shoulder, as if admiring the view, then take a step back and give a good nudge. Nothing to clean up or lug away, no anxious wait for toxicology. Nothing to do but call 911 and feign shock. Seeing him this morning, big as life in Blue Streak Coffee, made Nora woozy. It was his voice she recognized first, deep and easy, unchanged in 13 years. Behind him in line, she studied his backside—the fine fabric of his burgundy shirt, the tan cargo shorts, his well-muscled calves. When he turned to put a dollar in the tip jar, she saw the slight bulge above his eyebrows, the long straight nose, and she flinched. There he was. The man who killed her best friend.

"Marc," she said.

He wheeled around and looked at her, and she watched his puzzled expression morph into pleasure. Charming as ever, this one.

"Nora," he said, grinning. Veneers, she thought.

"What are you doing here?" The words came out more aggressively than Nora had intended, so she punctuated them with a hard, bright smile.

"Same-same. Looking at property."

"We're not going to get another mall, are we?"

He laughed, though she had not been kidding. "No. This is residential stuff—I'm checking out a couple homes for a buddy who's in Greece." He paused, scanned her up and down. "What's up with you? You look *great*."

It was true she appeared younger than her years. Of course, she worked on it, kept her weight down, her heels pumiced, her arms as firm as nature allowed. Nothing drastic, just steady effort. It did not feel like vanity so much as decency, taking care of the real estate she'd been handed—great legs, ample breasts, a face you didn't have to hide behind. Sheer luck, all of it. A favor you didn't forget.

"I'm okay," said Nora. "I live on Alta Vista now."

"Still writing?"

"Editing. It pays better."

"Are you married?"

"Was." Kurt, Nora's husband, had died in a plane crash.

"Kids?"

She shook her head. "What about you?"

"Two boys," he said, looking pleased.

Nora knew this. She also knew that his wife was a yoga instructor and that they lived in San Diego, where he sold commercial real estate. Through the Internet and updates from Joanie, a longtime friend, Nora kept tabs on Marc. Joanie still lived in Santa Cruz, but she and Marc were friends on Facebook, and so she saw his posts. When Nora visited Joanie they sometimes pulled up his profile page and clicked through the photos. Annika, Marc's wife, was blonde and lithe and looked a good deal younger than her husband. Julie died in September 2001. Marc married Annika in March 2003. Eighteen months, Nora concluded, must have seemed like a decent interval.

"When are you leaving?" Nora asked, again too abruptly.

"Tonight. I like driving at night—no traffic." He hesitated, calculating, then beamed at her. "Hey, how about dinner? Are you free?"

Recoiling, ready to say no, Nora reconsidered. This could be interesting. She'd watch his face, his every move. A consummate liar, he stood no chance tonight.

"Sure," she said. "What time?"

*

Nora pulled into the cracked driveway of her house, a brown-shingled 1960s bungalow draped with Monterey pines. She had moved into it when Kurt died, no longer wanting to live in the larger home they'd been happy in.

A first-time bride at the age of 39. That's life for you, finally stumbling on Mr. Right and losing him six years later. Most would agree that a quick death is better than a slow one, but Kurt's last seconds, in a small plane over the snowy mountains of Montana, had been spent in terror, and there was no consolation in that. Her bitterness stayed with her for months, until she was somehow able to get the upper hand, to wrest it into a box and out of sight. There it sat, she imagined, in the top of the bedroom closet, a constant companion to her husband's ashes. She and Kurt had never discussed final wishes, and as she could not scatter to the wind what little she had left of him, she would keep his remains, as well as her rancor, as long as she lived.

Nora opened the front door and stepped inside, gratified as always by the well-ordered space she lived in. The rooms were furnished like a doll's house: a sofa, a chair, a bed, a desk. There were a few nature photos on the walls—mossy forests, shimmering mountain lakes—and one savage philodendron that stealthily traveled the length of the windowsill as if looking for a way out. Nora was especially fond of the kitchen, built like a jewelry box, everything cleverly tucked away. A pocket bathroom separated the two small bedrooms, one for sleeping, the other for working.

Nora made coffee with the French roast beans she had just bought and sat down at her desk to work. It was a good distraction, honing someone else's words, and absorbed her almost as much as the creative writing she used to do.

She had spent too many years writing short stories and personal essays, most of which wound up in obscure literary magazines before falling into the oblivion of online archives. Recognition was scant, payment even scarcer, and so she was forever indebted to a teacher she met at the Santa Cruz Bookshop who steered her in a more gainful direction. This man did occasional editing for wildlife organizations and told her the pay was decent, the work steady. He was right about the money (better than you might expect), but the best part was the incidental knowledge, the wondrous glimpses into a world otherwise hidden. There was no practical value in assimilating this earthy information, no reason Nora needed to know that mayflies are the only insect with paired genitals—two penises for the male, two gonopores for the female—but the accumulation of these secrets became their own reward, layering her days with tenderness, the sense of herself as a breathing, pulsing participant. Here she was shifting paragraphs, changing syntax, while the world acted upon her in countless ways. She understood this now, could perceive the edifice, if only in fleeting pieces. Like every living thing, she was at risk, an evolving organism with limited control—maybe less control than anyone knew.

The article she was presently working on contained new research on parasites and the ways they alter the biology of their hosts. It was commonly believed that creatures flock or herd or school to better defend against predation—the safety in numbers theory. Possibly not, at least not in the case of brine shrimp. These creatures, Nora learned, were invaded by a tapeworm that turned them a tantalizing red, then urged them to swim as a group, making them easy prey for flamingoes—only in the body of a flamingo could this worm complete its life cycle. And brine shrimp were not the only creatures managed by wily invaders; all sorts of animals fell victim. There was a parasite, Toxoplasma gondii, nicknamed "Toxo," designed to reproduce in the body of a cat. To get there, it worked its way into rats and made them attracted to the smell of cat urine—bye-bye rat. Humans too were infected by this organism, about a third of the population in fact. Most of us were not noticeably impacted, but this latest study linked toxoplasmosis with certain mental disorders and even suicidal tendencies. How schizophrenia benefitted a one-celled parasite, Nora could not conceive, but given the diabolical complexity of life on earth, she assumed the damage was not incidental.

Nora worked until 4:00, then drew a bath and gratefully lowered herself into the steaming water. Normally she would have taken a shower, but today she wanted a nice warm soak, time to drift into her past, to bring Julie back to life.

Her family came from Golden, Colorado and moved to Santa Cruz when Julie was 12. The first time Nora noticed her was during show and tell in their sixth grade classroom. Most of the children had brought in things they'd found, interesting rocks or shells; one boy brought in a picture of his pet cockatoo—live animals were not allowed in school. Julie brought in a picture she had drawn, a polar bear standing on a lone ice floe, three white mountains in the distance. The bear was looking over his shoulder, and with just two dark spots, an eye and a nose, Julie had managed to make him appear bemused. Around his neck was the only splash of color: a striped scarf waving in the wind. The class had learned about polar bears the week before, how hard it was for them, out there on that ice, trying to find enough food for themselves and their cubs, and this bear, with his jaunty scarf, tugged at their hearts. The teacher, clearly impressed, gushed over the picture; the students merely stared at it, acknowledging their lesser skills (evidenced by drawings that hung from the classroom walls).

It would have been easy to despise a pretty new girl brimming over with talent, but Julie was hard to shun. After telling the class which brand of pencils she used and where to buy them, she invited anyone who was interested to come to her house and draw as a group. Her mother, she assured them, would furnish snacks. Nora gaped at Julie, charmed not only by her artless generosity, but by her long brown braid, her knee-high boots, her denim vest embroidered with small red horses, the earnest way she spoke. Was it that very next day they began walking to school together, talking for hours on end? It was like falling in love, Nora realized years later, swift and unstoppable. From nothing to bedrock.

Most of the time they hung out at Julie's house, which was filled with artwork in various stages of completion and smelled like oil paint and potpourri. Her father was a high school art teacher; her mother owned a business, American Yuletide. For three months each year, she traveled around the country buying USA-made Christmas decor, which she sold to retail stores. One of the bedrooms in the house served as her office, and it was always overflowing with cheerful samples: pinecone owls, tiny birch bark canoes, rabbits whittled from wood, fat red gourds turned into Santa's. Nora loved the time she spent in Julie's home, not just because of the treasures it contained but because the air was not thick with worry. Julie's parents, absorbed in their own pursuits, were polite and permissive, and Julie in turn gave them no trouble. It was as if the three of them had struck a deal, had agreed on a policy of non-interference, a home without punishment. Nora's house was different. Her brother was a 16-year-old alcoholic and her mother, a reluctant divorcee, worked long hours and seldom smiled. There was enough money, the place was reasonably clean, but you didn't want to be there.

On rainy winter days, Nora would sometimes pull out the photo albums in her office and study the years she had shared with Julie, from pea coats to hot pants, from Peter Frampton to Janet Jackson, from Toyota Corollas to Dodge Ram pickups. Together, combining theories, testing strategies, they made their way through school and beyond. Peering at pictures of her vanished friend—waving from the Giant Dipper, sunning on the beach in a gold bikini, disco dancing on her wedding day—Nora wondered what Julie would look like now. Would her eyes be hooded, her lips thinned, and if so, would she have altered them? At 48, would she be broad or lean, fit or not?

Nora could see them taking a yoga class together; discussing travel plans, their latest blood work, the pros and cons of cosmetic surgery.

Nora leaned back in the tub, gazed through the window at a pine branch and the gray sky beyond. The sun was gone, absorbed by a thickening fog.

The best thing about Julie, the thing that Nora missed most, was that she never talked rot. She meant what she said, hit the marrow every time. One clear morning when they were walking along the foamy shoreline, Julie casually remarked that she and her boyfriend Josh had had sex the night before. "The full version," she added. She and Nora were 17 at the time.

Nora stopped, gaped. "Wow," she breathed. "How was it? Worth the wait?"

Julie shrugged. "It was okay. Pretty good." She cast her gaze over the sun-spangled ocean. "Scale of one to ten, I'd give it a seven."

Nora considered this. "Maybe it'll be better next time. Maybe you'll reach ten."

"Oh, I already have," said Julie. "Lots of times."

Nora stopped walking. "With *who?*"

"With Josh," Julie said. "Heavy petting."

Julie knew her own mind, better than anyone Nora had ever met. One evening, stretched out on the twin beds in Julie's dorm room (they had both gone to UCSC), they started talking about life after college: what sort of work they saw themselves doing, what their homes would look like, what dog breed they might own.

"How many kids do you think you'll have?" Nora asked.

"None," Julie said. "Zip."

Nora sat up on the bed. "Why not?"

Julie thought about this a moment and said, "I guess because I can't imagine wanting them."

*

Nora did not have much time to get ready after her bath. Without thought, she pulled an outfit from the closet—blue blouse, linen pants—and quickly dressed, then ran a brush through her short blonde hair and applied a bit more blush, a fresh coat of lipstick. She reached for perfume, decided against it, slipped on a pair of sandals. For a few seconds she paused before the mirror, making sure there was nothing obviously wrong. Mirrors were crude tools, useful only for thwarting embarrassment—trailing slips, smudged mascara, spinach in the teeth; you couldn't ask any more of them. Mirrors were not eyes.

Marc and Nora had agreed to meet at Johnny's, a seafood place on the harbor. He hadn't been there, he said, but assured her he would find it. Nora drove carefully, slower than usual, observing the trees and pastel-colored homes, the streets overhung with power lines. Her stomach was tight, but she felt oddly calm, as if she were being directed to this assignation and knew there was no point in resistance.

She crossed the river, turned right onto San Lorenzo. Already some of the trees were turning; soon the town would empty out, would lose its brightly clad tourists and return itself to the locals.

In the beginning, there were no red flags. Nora began recalling their lives together years ago: Marc and Julie met at one of his open houses (Julie had wandered in, more curious than interested), and right away they hit it off, chatting about the home and its amenities, the advantages of the west side, what they liked best about living in Santa Cruz. At last she admitted that she was not a serious buyer, more a passerby, but Marc didn't care; he was already smitten, understandably so. Julie was a stunner—long wavy hair, shimmery brown eyes, a smile you wouldn't believe, and she carried that beauty with no effort at all, like she didn't even know it was there. Nine months later they were wed.

Everyone thought Marc was good for sensible Julie, that he loosened her up, made her laugh more often. Nora agreed. Marc was entertaining and certainly smart enough, and just the fact that Julie loved him gave him credence. Julie had been managing the grant program for the City Arts department, but seeing how much Marc enjoyed selling property, and how lucrative it was, she soon got her own real estate license and prompt employment in the company Marc worked for. As it turned out, Julie had a knack for the business and became one of the firm's top agents.

Nora drove on, recalling that brief, glorious era when they were all in their early 30s, partying every weekend, certain that life would only get better. For a second she could see Marc clearly: his close-set eyes, his modest lips, his jaw more sharp than square. She could not say what it was about his face that made it attractive. Maybe his appeal had nothing to do with his features and depended instead on the expression he wore, the satisfaction he seemed to exude, as if he were pleased with himself for no particular reason and pleased with you as well. And who didn't enjoy his wit, his fabulous mimicry? People hung around him, smiles at the ready, eager to hear whatever he offered.

Joanie was the ringleader back then and her spacious, messy beach house was where they gathered, to drink and smoke, talk and laugh, deep into the night. Joanie was on her second husband and seemed content, but Nora could tell she had a crush on Marc, albeit a harmless one. Even now she sang his praises, remarking on how well he had aged, how handsome his sons were.

Nora had never shared her suspicions about Julie's death, not with Joanie, not with anyone—what was the point? Her evidence was anecdotal, inadmissible, a rusted key in the middle of a field. And Joanie would not believe her anyway, would likely consider Nora a monster herself for suggesting such a thing. That's where people made a mistake—they kept ruling out the unimaginable.

*

Nora pulled into a parking space at the restaurant and sat for a moment, her heart beating fast. The sense of calm had gone away, left her on her own. She had no idea how she would act, what she would say. Before today, she had not seen Marc, had not spoken with him, since Julie's memorial service. In a quiet, stricken voice he had told her he was moving to San Diego, that staying in Santa Cruz would be too difficult. "I can imagine," Nora said. He gave her a hug and she stiffened in his arms, wondered who was waiting in San Diego.

Nora crossed the parking lot, bracing herself with the sharp salty air, and walked into the restaurant, glad to see it was not yet crowded. Marc wanted to be on the road by 8:00, and so she had made an early reservation. The host, a willowy blonde on blood red heels, showed her to a table alongside the window. Marc was not there yet; lateness was a habit of his, Nora remembered, for which, because of his charm, he was always forgiven.

She ordered a Grey Goose martini and spun it slowly on the cocktail napkin, admiring the pleasant room with its wood-paneled walls and view of the harbor. Below the hulking fog, every slip held a boat, and she spent a few moments reading the whimsical names: After Taxes, Pier Pressure, Seize The Bay, Aloan at Last. She took another sip, glanced at the door, frowned.

It happened during one of those raucous parties at Joanie's house. People were all over the place, out on the deck, sprawled in the living room, clustered around the neon-lit bar Joanie's husband had built. At some point the ice ran low and Marc offered to fetch more. Julie, lounging on the sofa, lovely in her bulky green sweater and black stirrup pants, regarded him dubiously.

"Are you okay to drive?"

"Absolutely," Marc said. He got to his feet and attempted to demonstrate his competence by walking a straight line across the braided rug. Nora, seeing his slight stumble at the end, rose from her chair. "I'll drive," she announced, though she was feeling flushed herself from two glasses of wine.

Christmas, five days away, made for a festive drive through the neighborhood. Icicle lights hung from the houses; reindeer and sleighs sprang from rooftops. One yard in particular blazed with cheer: palm trees wrapped in shining red ropes, elves hammering inside a shop, a doe and her fawn drinking from an ice blue pool, a big balloon Santa, waving at cars. "Oh wow," Marc murmured, and his warm boozy breath wafted Nora's way; it was not unpleasant. He turned to her, his face aglow in the sea of light.

"Can we to stop a minute?"

Nora pulled to the curb and turned off the engine, and for several moments they sat admiring the colossal effort.

"See the nativity scene?" Marc said, pointing. "The guy must have spent weeks on this."

Nora nodded. "And a fortune."

They had not sat there long before Marc reached over and laid a hand on her thigh. She looked down without surprise. It was not unusual, a hand on a thigh. Bodies took their chances—you couldn't blame them. Sometimes you got in the middle; sometimes you looked the other way.

It wasn't, Nora reasoned later, an act of total betrayal. There was touching, kisses. There was his mouth moving across her neck and collarbone, between her breasts. There was the hot damp of her jeans under his palm. There was his breath, and hers, coming faster.

At last she broke away, straight-armed Marc back into his seat. "This is crazy," she said, trying for a tone that would make light of the event, strip it of any consequence. She drew a fresh breath, turned the key and pulled away from the curb. Marc regarded her profile, then slumped back where he belonged. "Yeah," he murmured. "Crazy." They drove to the store without another word.

A drunken misstep, that's all it was; she had, after all, come to her senses. Still, the event sickened her, proved how common she was. There were some people for whom integrity was a reflex, people who cleanly avoided what did not belong to them, and then there were those for whom goodness was a daily challenge. Nora knew which group she fit into.

Two weeks passed before she and Marc saw each other again, at

Joanie's "New Year's Dissolution" party. Nora was ready for this meeting, was anxious to be done with it, to restore herself and Marc to their rightful places. Their trifling blunder would have no purchase; everything would be as it was.

He was in the kitchen, his back to her. "Hello, Marc," she said.

He turned around. "Hey there, you."

Before offering the customary hug, Nora met his gaze with a clear message, a look of shame and reproach and resolve. It never happened, this look made clear, and it would never happen again. But instead of returning this appeal with his own abashed regret, Marc answered with a different message: a wink and a sly grin.

Her face hardened. What did it matter that the error would not be repeated? Her pardon had been denied. She was now and forever his dirty little secret.

Would he ever tell Julie? Nora's heart sped up as she pictured a tell-all evening, Marc roused into righteousness, blurting his misdeed, taking her down with him.

Five stupid, sweaty minutes and here she was: chained to a creep.

*

Nora had finished her martini and was contemplating another when Marc arrived at the table. She had been gazing at the harbor and his appearance startled her.

"Sorry I'm late," he said in a rush, pulling out the chair. "Damn GPS took me for a ride."

"How often do you come up here?"

He sat down heavily, his cologne overwhelming the table, and Nora drew back, jarred by the proximity. Age was gaining on him: pouches under the eyes, cheeks starting to sag, three deep creases in his forehead. She looked a little higher and saw a perfect line of hair plugs.

"Not very often. Once a year or so."

All those years and not once had he tried to see her. Guilty bastard. "Do you ever see Julie's folks?" Nora asked, trying to keep the accusation out of her voice.

"I don't," he said, his voice apologetic. "I should. How are they?"

"Fine. He's retired, but Alexis still has her business."

The server arrived and Marc pointed at Nora's empty glass. "Another?"

"Why not?" she said with a shrug.

Marc looked up at the server, a thin boy with a goatee. "I'll have a Stoli over."

The boy darted off and Marc looked around the room approvingly. "Nice place. Good food?"

"It's okay." Marc picked up the menu and Nora noticed his wedding band, embedded in the skin around it. Everything about him seemed bigger now, though she wouldn't call him overweight.

"How's the real estate business?"

He lowered the menu and gave her a rueful smile. "A lot better than it was."

Nora nodded. "That must have been a wild ride for you guys."

"It was." He put down the menu. "Do you want an app? Want to split some crab cakes?"

"Sure."

"Think I'll get the sea bass. What about you?"

"Just a Caesar."

*

Nora wasn't very hungry after the crab cakes and two martinis. She barely touched her salad and did not care that the lettuce had rust spots and the croutons were hard as bullets. Marc, on the other hand, dispatched everything on his plate—the fish, the mashed potatoes, the skinny green beans, even the parsley. When he finished, he pointed his fork at her plate and told her that Barbie ate more than she did.

They talked about Santa Cruz and the ways it had changed; they talked a little about the work Nora did, the extraordinary things she learned. For several minutes Marc told her about his family and Nora pretended to listen. She did not want to hear about Annika and the boys.

"My husband died," she said. "A plane crash."

Marc's eyes widened. "Wow. I'm sorry."

"Something we have in common," she said. "Unfortunately." She looked at him squarely. "I miss him. I miss them both."

"I do too." And he did look miserable just then, his face long and sad. He had changed; he wasn't even funny anymore. Nora wondered if he ever regretted what he did, if he ever looked at Annika and wished she were Julie.

Regret. Guilt. Did people like him even feel these things? If he knew what Nora knew, about him and Julie, would he even care?

First off, Marc had never been a nature lover; his idea of a vacation was a long weekend in Las Vegas. The fact that he wanted to spend several days camping in Bryce Canyon came as a big surprise to Julie, who wasn't, by the way, sold on the idea. Julie was afraid of two things: German shepherds and high places. Would she have gotten that close to a cliff? And then there was the trouble at work. Julie was outperforming Marc and he resented her for it. He wound up changing companies and getting into commercial properties, but she still brought home more money. Their private life wasn't good either. For one thing, Marc wanted kids and Julie didn't. This was a problem that wouldn't go away. And then there was their sex life, or lack of it: Julie told Nora that Marc had no interest in making love, that he barely looked at her anymore. Nora didn't say what she was thinking: that if a 37-year-old man with a gorgeous wife loses his sex drive it's because he's parking in another lot—in this case a lot in San Diego, where he headed twice a month, supposedly on business.

And there was something else Julie mentioned, some sort of hot water Marc and a couple of his associates had gotten themselves into. She wished she'd never found out about it, Julie told Nora. Marc no doubt felt the same way.

As Nora was thinking about a way to prod Marc, to see if he would talk about Julie's death and if the details would differ now, he began speaking, his eyes fixed on the table.

"I didn't... I never heard her. I was looking at the map. When she didn't come back I got out and started looking for her. I kept calling her name. I ran all over that place, calling for her." His voice choked. "It was too dark by then."

This was true. Julie's body was not found until the next morning.

He paused, shook his head. "We were going to start fresh. No more messing around, no more lies. That's why I wanted us to get away. I wanted us to be someplace different so we could see what we wanted. We were going to get counseling." He swung his gaze back to Nora. "We were going to have a baby. That's what we were celebrating. We'd just left the restaurant."

His eyes were misted over now and bloodshot. She looked back up at his hair plugs, his fleshy, sagging cheeks. She almost felt sorry for him.

It was all plausible. At the age of 36, Julie may finally have decided to have a baby, if only to save her marriage; and whatever problems they were having in the bedroom may very well have stemmed from Marc's business worries; and maybe, spurred by courage or champagne or both, Julie had gotten too close to the edge.

And then there was Toxo. As long as she was looking at this from every angle, the fantastic could not be disregarded. If a tiny bug could hijack our will to live, maybe it could turn us against others, too. It was possible that Marc had not acted alone and could never account for what he had done.

Nora was a reasonable woman; she allowed for these alternate worlds. But people had to keep moving, had to build their arguments and live by them. The truth was up for grabs.

She looked at Marc, her face suffused with sympathy, and

reached across the table, placed her hand on his arm. "You poor dear," she murmured, and just as the gratitude softened his puffy eyes, she delivered a wink and a sideways smile. Just a little something for the road.

The Golden Age

Janie glared out the window at the trailer next to hers. Polly was taking a long shower and listening to Patsy Cline; she'd apparently taken her CD player into the bathroom and didn't care who was forced to hear it. Janie liked Patsy Cline as well as the next person, but not on a Sunday morning at 8:15 while she was doing yoga, or trying to. "Back in Baby's Arms"—how could she hold the mountain pose with that sailing into her living room?

She breathed in deeply, made room for her higher self. It was practice, she reminded herself, all these aggravations that came with life in a mobile home park. Who in their bright-eyed youth dreams of living in a trailer? These were places you found yourself in: no-fuss aluminum stalls in which to look back on the things you'd lost, through bad luck or poor choices or that waiting bandit, old age. This is where you went when stairs and repairs became too much, when your full-size home outgrew you.

Some made the best of it. Polly, for instance. Polly was game, Janie had to give her that, the whole-hog way she took on her little square of Destiny Park: fired up her mini Weber every Saturday night, filled her window boxes with vinyl geraniums, actually planted them in soil so they'd appear more real. She had installed a white plastic fence that handily snapped together, and she'd painted her walkway to make it look like flagstone, and though she had failed in this, though the stones looked like pink puddles, she was beaming when she finished. Seeing Polly standing back, admiring her work, Janie came out of her trailer and said, politely, "That looks nice." Polly wheeled around, gave her a big yellow grin. "It *does*, doesn't it? Came out better than I thought."

Janie moved into plank pose and held herself there for one full minute, counting off the seconds. Infirmity had not landed her at

Destiny Park, though given her age (82), some might assume this. Not that she didn't have her aches and pains—27 years of stunt work leaves reminders—but so far she had kept the upper hand with her body, putting it through its paces each day and buying the right fuel. She also drank more water than she wanted to and generally kept away from booze. You had to treat your body like the machine it was or you wound up tethered to trouble.

Only with Rick, in those two years they lived together, had she betrayed herself. They met at a party, or actually at the end of one, where they wound up in chaise lounges beside a moonlit swimming pool. "High Noon" was in production then, and Rick was doubling for Gary Cooper. Janie, who was still a newcomer at that time, was enthralled by the stories Rick told her that night, all sorts of thrilling things about the stars he worked with: those lines on Gary Cooper's face, that pained look? Well, he *was* in pain—the guy had a bad hip, back trouble and bleeding stomach ulcers. And Grace Kelly? She was hard on herself, thought her acting wasn't worth a damn. Janie was half in love by the time the sun rose over the Hollywood hills, falling hard for Rick's green eyes and slow spreading smile. He was a wild one, loaded with equal parts charm and Scotch. His voice was so deep that everything he said sounded reassuring, and Janie happily barreled down all the wrong paths with him. Eventually he drank himself out of the business, and if it hadn't been for Amanda, Janie might have followed. Her pregnancy kept her off the bottle, which is when she learned what a no-count bastard her boyfriend really was. Having no use for a knocked-up teetotaler, Rick rode off into the sunset, leaving Janie with the only thing he was good for: Amanda. Lemonade from lemons.

Rolling up her yoga mat, Janie saw that Coco, her long-haired dachshund, had come out of the bedroom and was now sitting head-first in a corner of the kitchen. She was doing this lately, mistaking corners for a way out; sometimes she sat in front of the hinged part of the door, no longer knowing how the door worked, where to position herself. At night she would often pace, her nails clicking against the linoleum when she reached the kitchen. "Coco," Janie would call out, "Coco, come sleep," and the clicking would stop as the dog paused in the dark, trying to figure out her next move.

Janie hadn't had her long, only four months. Coco had replaced Sam, who had replaced Sadie, who had replaced Kevin. Before these four, there had been Nova, the corgi she had when she moved in here. Janie had no idea she would wind up with all these senior animals. She'd had Nova 14 years, and the trailer was so empty afterward that she found herself at the pound a month later. Oh my, what a lot of dogs there were, most of them frantic, up on their hind legs, barking and whimpering, paws against the cages, tongues ready to lick any part you offered. Dogs of all shapes and sizes—basset hounds with German shepherd heads, greyhound legs on pitbull bodies. Some cages were overflowing with puppies from the same litter, squeaking, squirming bundles of joy. Those were the ones people wanted, the soft ones, the cute ones, the dogs with years ahead of them. Janie walked down the row and stopped in front of a grey-muzzled dog, some sort of terrier, that was lying in his cage, making no noise at all. "Hello," she said, and the dog rolled one cloudy eye her way but didn't lift his head. It was hard to tell if he had lost all hope or didn't care who took him. This dog was wise to humans, knew they couldn't be trusted. "His owner died," the attendant said. "We can't keep him much longer." So that's the one Janie brought home, the dog no one else was going to take.

There were some advantages, Janie soon realized, in adopting older dogs, especially if you lived in a trailer park. They didn't run anymore, so a pocket-size yard was fine with them. And they didn't gnaw your furniture or beg for a walk every two minutes. And, realistically, there was her own age to consider—she wouldn't want to leave a young dog high and dry. No, it was better to rescue the old ones. All they wanted was a quiet place to rest and someone beside them as their worlds closed in. It was so little to ask, really. They broke your heart of course, every one of them, but for Janie the pain was tolerable. If there was a limit to what the heart could take, she had not found it.

*

Janie and Coco reached the end of the lane and began to walk back. Janie had to slow her steps to accommodate Coco, who marched on stiff legs right beside her. That was another nice thing about older dogs—they did not require a leash. Coco would pause now and then to sniff the messages of other dogs, but she stayed on course, knowing her limitations. When she stopped to piddle, which was often, she would flatten her pelvis to the ground and peer about, checking for danger, and Janie, looking down, would be flooded with tenderness: this little red dog, this big wide world.

A steady breeze had cleared out the valley smog, and it was as perfect a spring day as anyone could want. Sunny, upper 70s, the snowy crags of Cucamonga Peak towering in the blue distance, below them a forest of palms trees. Say what you will about Los Angeles, how many people on the planet woke up to days like this?

And Destiny Park—it was better than a lot of others in the area. You had views, for instance, at least when you stepped outside, and most of the trailers were presentable. Everyone had an ample driveway; most had a shrub or two—stubby palms or Birds of Paradise. Real grass grew under the junipers along the roads, and here and there full-size trees had been planted. Probably the management was just trying to compete with the hundreds of other mobile home parks, but the greenery felt like a kindness. And they didn't have to contend with shrieking children either, other than the occasional carload of bored grandkids for whom the management had grudgingly supplied a small, rusting playground.

"Good morning, Janie!"

Theda waved from her deckchair. She and Nikki lived in a pale turquoise trailer directly across the lane from Janie's unit.

"Morning, Theda. Beautiful day." Janie stopped walking. Coco took the opportunity to sit, dropping her scrawny hindquarters and slumping to one side.

"Yes it is." Theda was a big-boned woman in her seventies with a cap of silver hair and a smile that involved her entire face. She and Nikki, who were a couple, had been living here for several years. When they were sitting outside in the evenings, their soft voices carried across the road, and Janie could often hear pieces of their conversation, pleasant patter about this or that. Occasionally they would laugh or vigorously agree on something, and Janie would pause and smile. What a gentle arrangement it seemed, growing old with someone who was aging in the same ways, drifting ever farther from the vanities of youth. When they cast a kind eye on the other's diminishments, did it help them love their own bodies more?

"Where's Nikki?"

"Making breakfast. Denver omelets and home fries." Theda leaned forward hopefully. "Would you like to join us?"

"I've already eaten," said Janie. "But thank you." The three of them dined together now and then, usually in Theda and Nikki's trailer, which was more spacious than Janie's. Their place was homey and welcoming, and they carefully avoided asking questions about Janie's personal life. They just wanted to hear about the stunts she'd done and what it was like to work in Hollywood in the fifties. Were Roy and Dale as nice as they seemed? Had she ever met John Wayne? They thought she must have led an exotic life.

Janie wouldn't call her life exotic. She had met plenty of movie stars, gone to plenty of parties, but her end of the business was not glamorous, it was arduous, especially for a woman. Men could wear padding under their clothes, but women didn't always have that option (especially these days when they were doubling for size two actresses, half naked and in high heels). Back in the 50s and 60s, movie sets could get pretty dicey; Janie had worked with a few stunt coordinators who were a lot more interested in glory than safety. Now the dangerous stuff could be animated; when Janie was working, the bodies were real. And you couldn't squawk, not if you wanted to keep working. The pay wasn't great either—stuntmen made a lot more than stuntwomen, and that, from what Janie had heard, hadn't changed.

How did she become interested in stunt work, Theda and Nikki wanted to know. What made her want to risk her life like that? Janie had pondered this herself; she couldn't remember a deciding moment. As a child she loved to jump off things, trees, sheds, anything in her path, and she liked going fast, liked to rocket through the neighborhood on her roller skates and ride her bike, no hands, down long steep hills. She could make a clean dive at fifty feet and swim farther than anyone she knew. By sixteen she had not outgrown this energy, and her mother's dismay, her ongoing entreaties, had no effect. Hoping to double for stars like Dale Evans and Jane Wyman, Janie started riding horses and working with trainers, and before too long her trick riding was good enough for auditions. It helped that she pretty and didn't make any trouble, and meeting some of the people Rick knew didn't hurt either.

"How's Coco doing today?" Theda asked.

"Oh fine," Janie said. "You know. She's a little stiff right now."

"Aren't we all?" Theda grinned. Gazing at Coco, her expression grew serious. "I don't know how you do it, Janie, taking in these dogs like you do." She had expressed these thoughts before.

Janie shrugged. "They're good company." She smiled at Coco, who gazed up at her with wrenching adoration. What did she see, Janie wondered, with those milky brown eyes? A face, features, or just a familiar blur? Her hearing was definitely getting worse; often she would startle, not having heard Janie's footsteps behind her.

Just then Polly's door opened, and she emerged from her trailer in a rush, her brassy hair already tumbling from its elaborate arrangement. She was wearing plaid Bermuda shorts and a pink tank top that strained across the grand shelf of her bosom. Her legs, which were in decent shape, glistened with an orangey tanning lotion that had turned her knees too dark. She checked the lock, then caught sight of Janie and Theda.

"Oh hi," Polly said with a quick wave. "Late as usual," she

apologized, hurrying to her car in precarious gold sandals.

"Hi Polly."

Janie, surprised by the male voice, turned her head. It was Al of course. Al Shiner. The park lech. He liked to do this, hang out in the shadows, then startle you with his creepy voice. He was standing beside his trailer, in a light blue bathrobe, holding a can of Coke. He hadn't shaved yet, and his hair—what was left of it—was sticking up on one side like a small dark horn.

Polly glanced over at him, too busy to mask a frown. "Hi Al."

Al had a thing for Polly, had been trying to find a way into her trailer for as long as Janie could remember. Pot-bellied, pushing eighty, he hadn't slowed down a bit, not as far as Polly was concerned. The fact that she was probably a generation younger and not the least bit interested had so far not deterred him. Which is something Janie had never understood about men: why they kept playing to an empty house.

Polly backed her red Impala into the road, and Al, his eyes narrowing with disappointment, watched her drive off.

"Ladies," he murmured, raising his Coke and climbing back into the darkness of his trailer. Given the rotted latticework, the sagging shingled roof, the rust stains coming off the gutter, Janie shuddered to think what the inside looked. Despite the covenants listed in the office, the park had a live-and-let-live policy, and loafers like Al took full advantage. Fortunately there weren't too many of his kind living here.

Janie turned back to Theda and said, "I'm going out later—do you need anything?"

"No, honey. We don't. We did a big shopping on Friday. But thank you."

"Well, enjoy those omelets," said Janie, who could now smell the onions and peppers cooking.

"Oh we will," Theda replied. "You have a good day."

"You too." Janie picked up Coco, who could not manage stairs, and carried her across the road and into the trailer, where, instead of cooking smells, there was the fragrance of sandalwood coming from the reed diffusers in the living room—it helped with the dog odor.

Janie's own breakfast had been modest: yogurt and a slice of rye toast with peanut butter. Only on Saturdays did she allow herself the sort of ranch-style breakfasts that Theda and Nikki consumed every morning. Janie actually admired them; there was bravery in giving yourself that much rope, especially at their age. Maybe it was her stunt training, all those years of planning and measuring and caretaking, but Janie had a firm grip on her reins and would not, could not, let them go.

*

Heading for Santa Monica, intending to spend the day at the ocean, Janie changed her mind and took the 405 north. Traffic was already thickening on I 10, and she knew the beaches would be crowded, the parking lots jammed. How much nicer it would be to wander the hills of Big Sky Ranch; she had a lifetime pass there and could visit any area they weren't filming in. She'd done several stunts at Big Sky, even doubled one time for Amanda Blake. They were the same age, same height and weight; all Janie had to do was pull on a red wig and get up the nerve.

Even before Gunsmoke went on the air, Janie knew that Amanda was headed for stardom. She was gorgeous, for one thing, the kind of looks people just gaped at, and she had this warmth about her, a whole-hearted love of everything. Amanda drew people in, she couldn't help it; they'd watch her laughing, enjoying herself, and pretty soon there'd be a crowd around her. Janie met her one night at Taylor's Steak House. She was sitting at a large round table, chatting and smoking (as they all did back then), her red hair and white shoulders gleaming, and when she looked up into Janie's eyes and smiled, Janie felt it right down to her toes. In no time at all, they became good friends, consoling each other or celebrating, whatever the occasion called for. The day Janie's daughter was born, Amanda was at the hospital, her arms overflowing with flowers.

One evening when Janie was watching Gunsmoke, her daughter, who was five at the time, walked over to the TV and put a finger on it. "Manda," she said.

"That's right. Did you know I named you after that lady?"

Amanda shook her head.

"Well I did. I knew you were going to be just like her. Pretty and strong."

And she had in fact grown up just that way. Amanda loved being on movie sets and watching her mother trick-ride; she listened closely to everything that was said and studied the careful way her mother approached each stunt, leaving as little as possible to chance. Despite this, Janie had her fair share of injuries—dislocated shoulder, cracked ribs, numerous sprains, bruises and cuts—all part of the business. Janie's favorite stunt was "horse boarding," where, standing up, she rode two galloping horses. "It's okay to be scared," Janie used to tell her daughter. "Fear comes with the territory. But you can't let it have the last word." It was no surprise to anyone when Amanda joined the Screen Actors Guild and began performing her own thrilling stunts—only hers were done on motorcycles, not horses. Sign of the times. Janie didn't like motorcycles, was bothered by their noise and speed. Of course there was nothing she could say.

No one was shooting at the Big Mesa lot, so Janie parked her car and began walking through the grassy meadows, bright green after the wet winter. Just she and the cows were out today, and she sat for a while under a massive oak tree and watched them graze. Off to the right, mirroring the sloping hills, was the near perfect circle of a manmade pond. Countless scenes had been filmed there, cowboys from Rawhide, Gunsmoke, The Big Valley, stopping to fill their canteens and water their horses.

Janie recalled the morning when a script required Miss Kitty to ride a horse, sidesaddle, down Dodge's main street. Amanda Blake was terrified of horses and begged to be taken out of the scene. They called Janie to come in and double, but by the time she arrived

Amanda was sitting on that horse. In her dogged way, she stayed there for hours, stayed as long as it took. After that, the only time Janie had to do any riding for her was a scene where Kitty's horse was obliged to gallop—the studio wouldn't allow their star to do that.

Nineteen years Amanda played Miss Kitty. When she finally left the series, people kept asking her why, as if two decades in the Long Branch Saloon were not enough. "Those swinging doors—I just couldn't walk through them anymore," Amanda told Janie, "couldn't wear that damn bustle *one more minute*." Her real interest, all along, had been animals (she wouldn't permit the use of any furs on the set of Gunsmoke), and up until she died, she spent her days working for animal organizations, creating refuges and leaving her entire estate to PAWS.

Gazing at the pond, remembering all this, Janie frowned. A woman like that, dying at 60, and from AIDS, of all things. The last time Janie saw her, she looked just awful. She knew she was going to die, but she was far more concerned with her animal retirement home. "I just hope word doesn't get out," she told Janie. "People might stop donating."

*

When Janie opened her trailer door, Coco rose from her bed beside the sofa—it took her three tries— and approached the kitchen, wagging her draping tail.

"Hi sweetheart," Janie said, squatting to stroke the dog's head and neck. Coco gave a low whine and gazed at Janie in boundless expectation. Her face was nearly white, though the flyaway hair on her long ears was still a reddish brown. With her short legs and long coarse fur, her body, lean as it was, barely cleared the floor.

"Dinner?" Coco lifted her ears and wagged her tail harder. Her appetite was not reliable, but the word itself excited her, as if it were a ball she remembered chasing.

Janie made Coco's food, as she had for all her dogs, boiling up assorted vegetables with ground turkey or beef. She could not imagine that canned food tasted very good, and anyway it was expensive. There were vet bills to pay, carpets and upholstery to keep clean.

She was not poor. She had worked in enough films to wind up with a modest pension, and there were the residuals, but when Art got sick, most of her savings flew away: first the ineffectual treatments, then the long-term care. And before the medical expenses, there had been the bad investments, ill-fated enterprises Art could not resist. Myopic in matters of business, he had been an adoring husband, and he spent loads of time with Amanda, standing in for her absent father. He bought a Harley Sportster just so he could ride with her, and he learned enough about motorcycle stunts to help her with the staging. When Art married her mother, Amanda was thirteen, that hormonal, impossible age, and it was Art's indulgent manner, the way he leaned in when he listened, that won her over.

Janie pulled a baggie of dog food out of the fridge, warmed it in the microwave, then poured it into a bowl. "Here you go," she said, setting the dish on the floor and standing back. Coco approached with caution, touching the food with her pointed nose and waiting a few seconds before taking a bite. "Good girl," Janie encouraged, and the dog looked up, the white crescents of her dark eyes showing, and took another small bite—whether she was genuinely hungry or just eager to please, Janie didn't know. Coco did manage to eat about a third of her meal before turning away and heading back into the carpeted living room, where she immediately slumped to a sit and waited for Janie to say or do something.

Not yet hungry herself, Janie drank a large glass of water while standing at the sink. Polly was back from her outing, and Janie had a clear view of her broad plaid behind. She was on her knees, planting red petunias in a clay bowl. A couple feet away was a new whirligig, a white horse with movable wings. There was no breeze at the moment, but it looked nice—better than the pooping dog she had stuck next to her fence.

Turning away from the window, she noticed that her answering machine was blinking: two messages. All those years of leaping for the phone when it rang, waiting for call-backs and jobs, and now she often forgot she had a phone. Polly, Theda, Nikki—they all had cell phones, as most everyone did these days, but Janie had skirted the need. Nor had she any use for a computer, no matter how handy they were: she was here, in person, and she wanted to see the world that way.

The first message was from her dentist—she had a cleaning on Monday. Along with the other parts of her body, Janie had been good about taking care of her teeth and still had nearly all of them. The second message was from a young woman who had gotten her number and was interested in interviewing her for an LA Times article. She wanted to write about Hollywood's golden age. Could they meet somewhere?

Janie walked into the living room, lifted Coco onto the sofa and sat down beside her. Coco immediately settled alongside Janie's leg and gave a sigh. All afternoon she'd been waiting for this, this small allowance; there was nothing more she required. Though she was slight enough to fit on Janie's lap, she did not venture there, nor did Janie encourage her to. People, animals, all creatures had a right to their limits.

For several moments Janie stroked Coco's fur and studied the photos on the opposite wall, some of which she'd taken herself. A smiling Dale Evans in her cowboy hat and embroidered shirt—Dale always dressed the part, figuring it reassured people. Barbara Stanwyck, surrounded by fans, holding court in front of a fireplace, arms waving imperiously. John Wayne and Maureen O'Hara on the set of Rio Grande, John standing tall in a cavalry uniform, Maureen glaring up at him, magnificently indignant. Susan Hayward stepping out of a cab looking beautiful and aggrieved—Susan was a cold one, never chummed around with the other actors after a shoot was over. Amanda Blake in boots, jeans and a flannel shirt, leg hiked on a fence rail, admiring the impalas she saved from hunting ranches. Agnes Moorehead as a Mongol in "The Conqueror"—now there was a bad movie, not just because it was awful, but because everyone on the set was exposed to the fall-out from atom bomb testing, and many of them, including John Wayne, knew it. Stunt people weren't the only ones risking their lives in Hollywood's golden age.

Janie would refuse this interview as she had all the others. Chatting with Theda and Nikki was one thing; divulging tidbits to a scandal-driven reporter was quite another. Though Janie had not been fond of every star she knew back then and could recall more than a few unsavory anecdotes, she was not inclined to offer them up as currency. These people were in their graves; they deserved some final respect.

On the table beside her was a close-up photo of Art taken at their wedding reception. People said he looked like Chuck Conner, and he did, before he got sick. That firm jaw, his keen, knowing eyes. He had a laugh Janie could hear now, one that came suddenly and all at once, a belly-deep guffaw. Amanda used to say he could blow a roof off with it.

Art had been good for Amanda, helped her have the sort of fun she too often denied herself. She'd been a serious child and had grown into a serious woman. "Focused" is what people called her, which of course she needed to be, riding motorcycles through mayhem at fabulous speeds. She was good at it, too, getting work in two major films and doubling several times on Charlie's Angels.

Coco was already sleeping. In the throes of a dream, her breathing quickened, her front paws twitched. Janie's thigh, where Coco's chin rested, was warm. When they were together, in a chair or on the sofa, Coco slept this way, her muzzle keeping a steady connection between them.

Amanda's pictures Janie kept in her bedroom, safe from questions or comments. She died at twenty-eight, practicing some elaborate motorcycle stunt, fortunately not in front of an audience. At once, Janie's world darkened, shrunk to a pinpoint, a tiny distant light far beyond her reach. She did not work, did not do anything but sit in a hard chair at her dining room table and think of all the things she had done, or hadn't done, that led to this fate. She had set the stage, bringing a fatherless child into the world, a child she could not adequately provide for, a child who was forced to spend more time with her grandparents than her mother. And though Amanda had plenty of love, and from so many, what a peculiar way to grow up. And later, what right had Janie to take her daughter to the studios, to take her on location, with all those cameras and cables and floodlights?

How close that other world had been! The one without the moonlit swimming pool, without Rick, without Amanda.

For a time she tried to live there, fending off the hurt, avoiding the pitfalls, but a world where Amanda had never been left Janie with nothing at all, and in the years that followed, to her slow surprise, she managed to find her way back.

Coco woke with a shudder, looked around in confusion, and then, seeing Janie's face, she settled down again and closed her eyes. Janie gazed at this small red dog she had brought into her home, a creature to whom now she was everything.

It was not an unreasonable arrangement. There was the having and there was the losing. Janie was not done with either.

Lovers and Loners

Coffee. That's all I've agreed to. One lean hour at Starbucks. She'll want more of course, but I need to hold onto my day. This is a mission—get in, get out.

I can thank my brother for this. Not that Tanner knew he was dumping his ex-wife on me, that I'd be haunted with her phone calls and emails for the last seven months. That I'd become the prisoner he used to be.

"Why did you ever marry her?" I asked him. "You couldn't see she had a problem?"

What he saw, Tanner explained, was a pretty girl who loved every inch of him. Yes Daria could be overzealous, and yes she cried easily, but these, he thought, were feminine qualities, proof of her passion and sincerity. He did not see them as problems. A year into the marriage he knew he'd made a mistake, but it took him two more years to get away: every time he summoned a smidgeon of resolve, she saw it coming and took him in her arms, reminded him of her steadfast love. She'd look up at him, tears already spilling from her blue doll eyes. Stay, they said. Don't leave me. When Daria was nine years old her mother met a cattle baron from Costa Rica and wound up moving to his ranch, leaving her Sacramento home and stunned family behind. Daria had "abandonment issues," a condition she readily disclosed—fair warning for those canny enough to heed it.

That's life, right? People come and go. I was dumped, too. Twelve years into our marriage, Russell told me he was gay. "I've slept with men," he added in a somber voice, as if the term was foreign and needed explanation. He leveled his earnest gaze at me. "Safely. I've always been safe."

I hadn't a clue. Russell was well-groomed, a snappy dresser, but this did not strike me as evidence. Not until his confession did the dots start connecting themselves. *Of course*, I thought, recalling the biographies in his office: Rock Hudson, Montgomery Clift, Oscar Wilde; then there was the way he assessed quality—shirts, furniture, bed sheets—by running his hand over the fabric, a skill I did not possess; and the way he loved high heels, the look of my legs when I wore them. My breasts, which are equally flawless, he ignored.

He fooled me in bed, too. Not that he was ravenous, and certainly not adventurous (he drew his lines, darn it), but I don't recall any performance problems. Little did I know just how good those performances were.

"Maybe you're bi," I said. I wasn't arguing; I was confused. But he shook his head slowly, regretfully, and I knew that decisions had been made without me. I looked at his close-cropped hair, reddish-brown, tidy as a bird's breast, and thought how much I would miss this feature, this daily gift I had lived with so long. We would remember each other in snapshots, in pieces. He would miss my legs; I would miss his hair.

Turned out he'd fallen for someone, a planning commissioner from Thousand Oaks; Russell moved into his house not long after the divorce was final. I made out well in the settlement (Russell was generous, as I knew he would be), and I was not irreparably wounded by his defection. Discovering your spouse is gay knocks you sideways. At first you question all your instincts; you're not even sure what kind of bread to buy. But then, one clear November morning, you look through your kitchen window at the palm fronds flashing in the sun, and you realize all at once that you are exempt, blameless. There was no battle, there were no victors. You were not unseated by a better, prettier version of yourself, but by a soft-spoken, pot-bellied man named Larry, whom you have actually come to like.

Daria is waiting at a table near the back of the store. When she sees me her face lights up and she springs from her chair. If she were a dog, she'd be piddling on the floor, whacking her tail against the table legs. Immediately she wraps me in a smothering hug—she's gained a lot of weight since Tanner left. Funny how grief whittles some people and bloats others. I lost 12 pounds when I found out about Russell, pounds I didn't need to lose. Knowing what was good for me, I put them back on, drank Ensure till it ran out my ears.

"Gina! You look *great!*" she cries. "How *are* you?" She talks like this, punching too many words, another exhausting habit of hers.

"Good," I say, settling my coat on a chair. She pins me with a huge helpless smile and I look away, pretend to read the menus on the wall.

"We don't have to eat here," she says. "We can get coffee, then have a real breakfast. Maybe IHOP?" The chances, she knows, are slim to none, but she leans in hopefully.

"No. I just want a latte and a croissant." I say this firmly, in a manner that borders on rudeness—believe me, it's the only way.

"You want another?" I ask, pointing to her coffee. "A muffin or something?"

"Just coffee." With a guilty upward glance, she adds, "My sugar's kind of high." She reaches for her purse and I wave her off.

The line isn't too bad. I glance over while I'm waiting and see her sitting there, waiting like a good dog, Even though her back is to me, I see the eagerness, the barely controlled energy. When I return to the table with our coffees and an almond croissant, she beams at me and, as if there's no time to lose, immediately starts talking.

"I took your advice. I joined that writers' group. We meet once a month."

"Good for you. How many members?"

Daria pauses, purses her little red lips. "Thirty? About half of them are *men*." She grins, her shoulders squeezing together like a child's. These are better odds than she encountered in the birders' group. It was my idea that she join a club instead of wasting any more time on online dating sites. Her profile, posted on Match, eHarmony and OkCupid, had chummed up only two prospects: one man collected large dolls and would not eat sitting down; the other was looking for a woman to share his underground survivalist fortress in rural Utah.

"A lot of them are, you know, older, but that's okay. I don't mind that." And she goes on at length about the people in the group and which ones she finds interesting, and then she mentions that most of the men want to write their memoirs while the women want to write stories. That figures, I think. Men want to plant a flag, make solid their existence. Woman prefer alternatives: places they didn't see, people they might have been.

I bite into my croissant and it surrenders in my mouth, melts into what it's made of. I have the constitution of a musk ox and could eat these bundles of butter three times a day without harm. My body, that's where all the luck went, my legs and bust and bulletproof blood. My face is where the compromises came in, as if God had spent too much on the framework and had to cut corners on the facade. I have a long nose, and my eyes, though large, are not lovely. Euphemistically you might say I have an aristocratic face, a face you might, over time, find some value in. On the street you wouldn't give me a second look.

"We have homework," Daria says. "We're supposed to write for 20 minutes without stopping or changing anything."

"Freewriting," I say, picking up my coffee. "Silences the inner critic."

She cocks her head, smiles admiringly. "How do you *know* these things?"

"I took a class in college. So have you tried it?"

She shakes her head. "Not yet. Maybe tonight."

"Does it interest you? The class, I mean. Do you like to write?" I want to stay with this topic, to talk about anything other than her failed marriage. For weeks Tanner is all we talked about, even though all I ever did was bounce her queries back at her. Tanner had never been one to share his feelings, I told her, but she would not give up. Each time we spoke she'd ask the same questions, as if with just a little more effort I might remember something valuable. Why had he left? Had he said anything to me? Did I think there was a chance they would get back together? Had he fallen out of love? What she wanted was confirmation, something her fears could feed on. She wanted me to look straight at her and break her broken heart: *Daria, you are too much. You are quicksand.*

It's a shame too, because otherwise she is fine. Otherwise she is a nice person who works in a dental office and pays her bills and takes care of her things. Every year she does charity walks and seems genuinely happy for other people and their accomplishments, and while she doesn't aim very high, she is not stupid. I sometimes wonder what she might have been were it not for this affliction.

Daria lifts her coffee, and I notice her puffy fingers and perfect nails. Nice fingernails impress me, especially on someone so flimsy— I bite mine. There is still a white line where her wedding band was; only recently, at my suggestion, did she surrender the stubborn squatter. I don't know if she was wearing it out of defiance or hope, but I reminded her that it might be a problem for would-be suitors.

She used to keep a diary, Daria tells me. She hopes this class will get her inspired. I nod encouragement, tell her that recording her thoughts each day might be useful, might help her make sense of things.

"Do you?" she asks.

"No," I admit. "But I should." And I mean this. Written accounts have value beyond measure—look at our desperate efforts to translate ancient tablets. I have a fear that one day when I am old, I will look for clues to my youth and find an empty vault. Photos only tantalize, they never yield enough.

There is a small commotion at the table next to us as three people and one guide dog settle in. The dog, a harnessed golden retriever, assumes his post beside the chair of his owner, a woman with red hair and crimped eyes. They are accompanied by an older man with a handlebar mustache and a lanky teenage boy. The boy immediately refers to his cellphone; the man looks over at me and smiles lightly, a courtesy I return. The woman is young—in her twenties, I'd guess—and I wonder if she's ever seen anything at all, and then I wonder, like I always do, which would be worse: blind from birth or blind from a later date. I smile at her regardless, letting the goodwill fall where it may.

Daria looks up from the dog. "I wish you could pet them," she says. "I want to. It's kind of unfair to the dog, don't you think, that no one can touch it?"

This is what I mean about Daria: she's a caring sort. One minute I'm clawing to get away from her, and the next minute I'm feeling bad about it, the same bind my brother was in.

I regard the dog who returns my gaze without interest. "I wouldn't worry, " I say. "I'm betting that dog gets plenty of love."

"Do you still have that hamster?" Daria asks.

"Hedgehog. Yes. It's a girl, by the way."

"How do you know?"

"You put them in a glass dish and look at them from below. The males have a big belly button—only it's not a belly button." This is the only way to sex a hedgehog. They are very private animals and will clamp themselves into a ball if you try to examine their undersides. I learned about the Pyrex trick on the Internet.

"What are you going to do with it?"

"I'm keeping her. I call her Garbo," I add with a grin. "She prefers her own company."

Daria gives me a puzzled look. "What does Garbo mean?"

"*Greta* Garbo?" Daria's expression does not change. "She was an actress," I explain. "A famous one. She became a recluse." Daria is only ten years younger than me and has lived in Studio City since she was twelve, and while you might think she'd know who Greta Garbo was, I'm not surprised she doesn't. Some people live that way, immune to the periphery.

Daria nods with polite disinterest, and then says, "Isn't it weird, the way that guy just left?"

I give a gust of contempt. "I'd call it monstrous." What sort of creep abandons an animal, leaves it for the janitors to deal with? This guy, Adam Starkey, lived in the unit right across from mine. He was a real spook, never talked to anyone. About a month ago I was on my way to the parking lot and saw a couple young men from the Pasadena Cleaning Service pulling furniture out of his condo. Tom Chase, one of the managers, was there and told me that Starkey had left him a voicemail the night before, said he wouldn't be back and they could take what they wanted. "Look at that," Tom said, pointing to a badly stained recliner with a wretched cage on top of it. "There's some kind of animal in there. You want it?"

As you can imagine, Garbo wasn't doing very well. She was sluggish and her eyes were running, and she wasn't breathing right. I called a couple vets, who offered to euthanize her for free, but I couldn't do that. And I didn't want to risk a Craig's List ad, fearing she'd wind up in some awful place filled with screaming kids and nosey dogs. So I took her in, bought her a nice new cage, the biggest I could find (the one she was in was filthy and too small—the poor thing had been more hostage than pet). Of course I had to read up on hedgehogs, had to find out in a hurry what they need; hedgehogs aren't like hamsters; they aren't like anything. After she had stopped panting and was moving around again, I lifted her from her cage one morning to get better acquainted. Right away she clamped up, her spiny back tickling my palm, and peered at me, her clawed paws tucked under her cheeks, her nose faintly twitching. Hedgehogs have poor vision, and I don't know what she saw, my features or just a blur. She seemed calm, maybe resigned. All I could fathom in those dark bright eyes was bewilderment, as if she were amazed to find herself back from the brink. I had a hard time believing it myself. I own a sweet shop; I make cupcakes for a living. Who knew I could be useful?

I tell Daria about Garbo's recovery, what measures I had to take: the ceramic space heater I had to buy, the special bedding; how I had to handle her each day so she would start to trust me.

"What do hedgehogs *do*?" asks Daria. "Why do people keep them?"

I don't know. Why do people keep anything? I finish chewing and say, "Company, I guess."

"Are they like cats? Do they sleep in your lap?"

I shake my head. "Garbo sleeps in her igloo. I bought her all new stuff: cage, igloo, water bottle, food bowl." I pause, notice Daria's rapt expression. This is another feature you have to admire, the way she listens; not a lot of people give you that.

"And an exercise wheel," I add. "She didn't have one. I hear her at night, spinning away—they can go ten miles at a time."

Daria grins. "I wish *I* liked to exercise that much."

"Me too," I sweep the fallen flakes of croissant into my hand and dump them into my empty coffee cup. "Nobody knows why rodents love those wheels. If you put one out in a field, the wild mice will start using it."

"That's *amazing*," Daria murmurs.

"When she's not on the wheel, she's either sleeping or rummaging around her cage, snorting like a little pig, looking for food. I give her cat food, a few veggies—peas, grapes. Sometimes I drop in a bug." Which is what she'd be eating, bugs and worms, if she were where she belongs. With a hedgehog, with anything in a cage, you do the best you can; you try not to think about the natural order of things. I live in a huge hive of apartments in east L.A., buzzing in and out like everyone else under the mantle of smog our cars create. There's nothing natural about our lives either.

My hand is in my lap, and even though I am sly as I can be about checking the time, Daria knows I just looked at my watch. Her eyes widen; even her hair goes on alert. Once again, I am struck by how much she looks like a doll: the springy coils of blonde hair, the apple cheeks, the red triangle of lips, those odd blue eyes that seem lit from behind.

Daria sits back, strategizes. Our hour is nearly up, and this is the point she will start to toss roadblocks my way, grabbing anything she can find. Her face brightens when she remembers my job.

"How's the cupcake business?"

"Good. I'm doing a wedding in the Palisades next week. They've ordered five hundred minis. Yellow rose frosting with a small purple rose on the side." My business is called Cupcakes At Your Door. I started it six years ago with two women I met in Starbucks. The first couple years we barely broke even, trying to figure it all out, but now we're turning jobs down. With all the bad press about wheat and sugar, you'd think the phone would stop ringing, but no. People will always allow for fun, and that's pretty much what cupcakes stand for. Someone told me once that beer, candy and flowers are the three inviolable commodities; you can add cupcakes to that list.

Daria shakes her head, sighs deeply. "Oh I wish I could eat cupcakes. I'm not supposed to." She frowns. "I can have the sugar-free version, but they don't taste the same."

"No they don't." I say. "That's why we don't offer them." I thought we should at one point, but when I learned that sucralose was discovered while someone was doing pesticide research, I shelved the idea.

This has actually been a painless hour, even pleasant. I'm glad we had the writers' group to talk about, and Garbo. I even have hope that Daria is finally spreading her wings, but just as I'm lifting my purse from the back of the chair, cueing my departure, she asks in a quaking voice if I've seen Tanner. *Damnit.*

"Not lately," I say brightly, opening my purse and peering into it to avoid Daria's eyes. "He's pretty busy."

Tanner works in construction. He has the effortless kind of physique that comes from hard labor, the sort of body you'd see on a Chippendale dancer. If he's the least bit aware of it, you'd never know; naturally women swarm him. For a long time he wasn't dating anyone, but last night when he came for dinner he told me about Mona, a veterinarian he's been seeing. "Sounds serious," I said. He took a pull from his beer, gave a shrug. "I like her." I hope Mona doesn't expect too much: Tanner says he's never going to get married again and I accept this as the truth.

When I look back up at Daria, her eyes are brimming over with tears, as I imagined they would be, and I see that any progress she has made would fit inside an electron. I don't say anything, for there is nothing new to say. In a moment she will stop and wipe her eyes and tell me she's okay, and I will pretend to believe her. This time she surprises me.

"It was easier for you," Daria says, a tear spilling down each cheek. "Russell left you for someone else, he left you for a reason." She pauses, pulls a Kleenex from her purse. "Tanner just *left*."

I had no idea she had made this distinction, was using it as an argument against herself. Why didn't I see that? If there's blame to be assigned, Daria will raise her hand every time.

"Tanner doesn't know what he wants," I counter, defending my brother with a lie. "And by the way, there was nothing easy about my divorce—hell, I drove my husband to another *gender*."

Daria reaches out and squeezes me arm. "I'm sorry. I really am. I know it must have been hard. I don't know why I said that."

"The point is," I say, more gently, "I was wrong. What happened to Russell had nothing to do with me, and it's the same with Tanner." She has stopped crying and is examining my face so closely that all I can think of is a big yellow dog, ears lifted, waiting for a bacon treat. She wants clues, hunches; she'll take whatever nuggets I give her.

"His leaving? That was all him, Daria. He's confused. He's just drifting now." I hate to say this, knowing how she will construe it, the phony hope it will bring, but I can't think of anything else to say and I really need to go. One day I might have enough time and nerve to tell Daria the truth, that Tanner left because he couldn't breathe, but now I just need to free myself.

As always, she throws herself in front of me, blocks the exits. Do I want to check out the new health food store with her? What about the Getty—the gardens, she heard, are *perfect* now. "No can do," I tell her, getting to my feet. "Next time." The blind woman tilts her head our way; she knows what's going on.

Daria enfolds me in a hug so long and hard you'd think I was dying. I pat her broad back and tell her we'll talk soon, and she gives me a quivery smile, says she'll call next week, and then I am on the outside, the world opening up around me.

I hope Daria finds someone in her writing group, maybe some older man who needs that kind of attention. It occurs to me then that Daria might make an excellent nurse, fussing and cooing, listening at length. She has that kind of patience.

At any rate, it's the only way she'll get over my brother, which is true of most people— exes sit on blocks in the driveway until a new love hauls them off.

It was different for me. Oh, I looked around, went on some dates, even slept with one of my supply reps a few times, but we didn't start any fires. It's been ages since I went down that road, and honestly? I just don't have the interest. Romance is something I seem to live fine without. We don't all come in pairs.

Take Garbo. One of the first things I wanted to do was buy her a buddy. The idea of her living alone for the five or six years she has, never seeing another hedgehog, pained me. I thought a nice female companion would be perfect, would at least not be jumping her every minute (maybe). Fortunately I did my research first.

Hedgehogs live alone, crossing paths rarely and only long enough to mate. No matter what combination, two hedgehogs in the same cage will begrudge each other, often battling to the death; at the very least there will be food fights, wheel wars.

Sometimes at night when I hear Garbo spinning, I come into the room and watch. She doesn't pause to look at me, doesn't care I'm watching. This is her time and she can't give it up.

Happy Hour

Roni picks up her vodka tonic, takes a long swallow, wipes her mouth with the back of her hand.

"I wasn't sure what it was at first," she says, setting down her glass. "I thought it might be a turtle. But then it swam up close and stopped, maybe ten feet from me, and I saw it was a river otter. I smiled. I thought it wanted to *play*. 'Hello there,' I said, or something like that, and it growled."

She shakes her head. "Yeah, that scared me. The otter went under then—I could see the water swirling towards me. I started backpedaling. The next thing I knew, it was biting the hell out of my legs."

"Oh my god," I breathe, "that must have been horrible. What did you do?"

"Screamed. Kicked. I tried to push it away—that's how this happened." Roni holds up her left hand; half her little finger is gone. I had been wondering about that.

"I got bit about a dozen times." She pulls up her pant leg to show me, and I notice she has stopped shaving her legs. Sure enough her calf is riddled with scars: punctures and a couple dark crescents. "There's one on my thigh that took fourteen stitches."

I peer at her leg, look back up. It's been a long time since I've seen Roni, and studying her today is a pleasure I wasn't prepared for. Like most women who are good-looking in their youth, she has grown more striking, as if now that her beauty is fully formed, she has taken possession of it. I would recognize that face anywhere, though much about her has changed. Her skin is very tanned for one thing, not those orangey tans you bake or spray on, but a weathered tan that shows the white laugh lines around her eyes. Her dark hair, which she used to wear in a long smooth braid, is now short and choppy. She is bigger, too, filled out with muscle; her arms are spectacular in that lime green tank top. What surprises me most is her smile—there's an upper tooth missing on the side of her mouth; I can't stop focusing on it. How long has she let that go?

"Jesus, Roni. How did you get away?"

"Someone in a boat heard me and zoomed over. They smacked the water with a paddle till the otter swam off. I had to get rabies shots."

"Ewww. In your stomach?"

"No, they don't do it that way anymore. Still hurts though. They give you shots in your hip when you come in, and then you get five more in your arm over the next month."

"So they knew the otter was rabid?"

"No. You can't tell if an animal is rabid unless you test its brain tissue." She frowns. "I don't think it was rabid, I think it was just protecting its young." She lifts her drink and takes another swallow. "Otters have their pups wherever they can find cover—piles of driftwood, old beaver dens, log jams. I'd been fishing near the shoreline, near this huge fallen tree. I got hot, so I dropped anchor and went for a swim." She flashes a grin, and the gap in her teeth comes back into view. "Wrong time, wrong place."

*

You could say the same thing about me and Roni. Who knows how long we might have lasted if Becca hadn't shown up? Roni and I weren't in love, but we may have wound up there; we laughed a lot, and the sex was—well it was pretty much all we did, wherever we could.

There's more than one way of falling in love: It can be subtle or swift; you can fall or you can hurtle. Becca came like a detonation, wiping out everything around me in ever-widening shockwaves. Roni was the first casualty, followed by my friends and plans. I even sold my fish tanks because Becca said they made the living room smell like a swamp.

Now, thirteen years later, Roni and I are back together, at least for the afternoon. Not long after Becca took over my life, Roni moved back to Duluth to help her father recover from a stroke. We kept in contact for a few years, then fell out of touch. Yesterday she called me, said she was back in town for a couple days and did I want to have a drink. The news made me giddy, made me smile into the phone. For several months of my life, this woman had merged her days and nights with mine. Our memories of that time, pleasant or painful, rose from the same ground. She is more than my ex, she is proof of my youth.

We are sitting at a table in Vitus, my favorite bar in Berkeley. It's cool and dark in here, and not too loud, especially at this time of day when people are still at work. Above our table is a faintly glowing sconce shaped like a dolphin. Ancient Roman scenes bloom on the walls: orators in togas on grassy hillsides; women sponging each other in public baths; men sprawled on stone couches, drinking from chalices, rings of ivy around their heads. The smooth voice of Norah Jones drenches the room: *"I love you when you're blue, tell me darlin' true, what am I to you?"*

"So when did you get interested in wilderness survival?" I ask. That's what she's been doing, she told me, teaching women how to stay alive in the wild.

Roni pauses, her face turning pensive. There's some grey hair in her temples now that makes me feel tender. I remember those dark eyes and high cheekbones, the shadow cleft in her chin. She still has great lips.

"I guess it started with that otter," she says. "I kept thinking about how fearless it was, how ready." She looks at me in earnest, her cheeks flushed, probably from the drinks. "Leah, can you imagine living like that? Engaged in every *minute*?" The idea sends a hopeful thrill up my spine: I am thinking about Roni, not the otter.

"Not really," I say.

She sits back, spins her empty glass on its coaster. Wrapped around one of her fingers is a bright blue Band-Aid. Her hands look older than she does.

"I wanted to feel that way—fierce, you know? I'd never fought for anything, not really."

"You were a badass landscaper," I remind her. When Roni and I were dating, she worked for a landscaping company that used no power tools; everything had to be cut, pried and dug by hand. Sometimes at night her arms would tremble with fatigue; I could feel the muscles twitching under my palms.

Roni shoves a hand through the air. "That was just work. Dumb work. Now I'm doing something I love."

"What's your company called?"

Her shoulders go back in pride. "Wild Ways."

"Great name. Business good?"

She nods. "It's really picked up since Gwen (her sister) made me a website—I can't do any of that stuff. Can't even figure out this thing half the time." She pulls her cell phone out of her back pocket.

"Most people consider *that* a survival tool."

She snorts. "Try building a fire with it."

"So what brings you out here? Did you fly?"

Roni shakes her head. "Drove. I'm heading up to Oregon tomorrow. I'll be teaching in Bend till the end of November. Weekend classes, immersions, too."

"What are immersions?"

"No tents, no sleeping bags. You gotta be butch for those," she says with a wink.

I don't even like to camp, ever since that Tahoe trip. Not long after we met, Becca and I went there for a long weekend, drove out to a remote area and hiked all day through grassy meadows and pine woods. Didn't see a soul. We pitched our brand new tent near the edge of a small lake, lit a fire, then laid outside in our sleeping bags and looked at the sky. There were so many stars, meteoroids too, falling to earth in neon green streaks. After a while we both dozed off, then a noise woke me, a soft crackling sound—I thought it was a bear or deer. The fire was still going, and I looked over it, and there was this man standing at the edge of the woods staring at us. "Get the gun!" I yelled (we didn't have a gun). Becca was on her feet in an instant. We saw him hightail it into the woods, and then we started throwing stuff into the car. I poured the thermos water over the fire, Becca jumped behind the wheel, and we tore out of there, didn't talk, just drove, all the way to Tahoe City. We spent the rest of the night in the Subaru in a Safeway parking lot.

I tell Roni this story, finishing with, "So that's why I'm not a big fan of sleeping in the great outdoors."

She leans across the table and says, pointedly, "That's exactly why you should take a course. It's not just about fires and shelters— it's about empowerment. That's why I love teaching this stuff to women." She clamps her hand over my wrist. "I'm telling you, Leah, you gotta get past that man in the woods."

*

Roni's reaches for the menu, asks me if I'm hungry; I'm not, but I order something anyway so she won't feel self-conscious. While we're waiting for the food to arrive, she gives me a few survival tips. The watery syrup from a maple tree, she says, is nature's energy drink. You just make a gouge in the bark and drink up. I also learn that cattails are edible—when the tops are young you can eat them like corn dogs, but the best part is the white stem close to the ground. The horns of a crescent moon can point you in a southerly direction, she says, and if you know just one knot, it better be the bowline, which she demonstrates with two cocktail straws.

I watch and listen closely, fascinated by these things Roni knows, by what she has become—a meat-eater, for one thing. When we were dating, she refused to eat anything with fur or feathers; I guess all that time in the wild has brought out the hunter in her. I almost question her about this but decide it's none of my business. I also stop myself from making a joke, asking if she prefers squirrel to beef, because I don't know if she'd find that funny, and if all I get is this one afternoon with Roni, I'm not going to blow it. So I just sit back and watch her eat her cheeseburger, which she does with obvious enjoyment, and let my mind sneak back to the places it wants to go, like the first time we slept together. We'd been shooting pool and flirting, giving each other The Look, brushing arms as we passed, and sometime after midnight we left the bar and made a beeline for my apartment. Once we got there, I was willing but shy, uncertain how to proceed. I hung up our coats and turned on the television, and Roni walked right over and turned it off. I think about that night, how fun and easy it was, and I wonder if, given the chance, our bodies would remember each other, would fall back on their own muscle memory and effortlessly resume, with or without us.

Roni polishes off the last of her French fries and nudges her empty plate to the side—she ate the orange slice, and the rind; she even ate the sprig of ruffled parsley. I am still picking at my salad, too keyed up to eat.

"I've been blabbing away," Roni says. "What's up with you? You still with Becca?"

I smile ruefully. "We really need to keep in better touch. Becca moved out three years ago—an ugly surprise."

Roni slaps the table. "I told you she was a bitch!" she crows.

I laugh at this, mainly because Roni said no such thing. She was actually a gracious loser, slipping out the back door of my life without protest. In fact, she behaved so decently that if I weren't stunned by Becca at the time, my feelings might have been hurt.

"I used to see her around town but not anymore," I say. "She moved her practice to Piedmont—the women are older there, and they have a lot more money." Becca is a plastic surgeon.

"Gotta tell you," Roni says, "I always thought she was kind of an ass—that long leather coat she always wore, the way she shoved up her collars."

I nod, remembering. "She never stopped doing that—she even did it with her pajamas." We both get a laugh out of this.

"Are you with anyone now?" Roni asks. If there is anything more than polite interest in her voice, I can't detect it.

I shake my head. "No one. I dated a grief counselor for a while, but she got weird, started hanging pictures of angels on her walls. She was more interested in the afterlife than this one." I push my salad aside and start folding my napkin. "After 40, the pond pretty much empties out, have you noticed?"

Roni gives a firm nod.

"Each time I meet someone," I continue, "I wonder what's wrong with her, why she's alone. They're not dates anymore, they're suspects." Roni tosses her head back and laughs, that full-on whooping laugh, and for an instant I am back there, where we were. "What about you," I ask. "Are you with anyone?" I hold my breath, hoping she is single, that we are comrades.

"Nope. I was with a woman named Suzanne for a long time. She died a couple years ago—skiing." Roni says this flatly; I can see she does not want to elaborate. "I haven't had much interest since."

Now I feel terrible. "I'm sorry. That's awful."

Roni shrugs. "It was, but I'm good now. Having the business helps," she adds. "Are you still working for that CPA firm?"

For many years I worked in the reports department of a large accounting firm in San Francisco. The only challenge of my job was overcoming the boredom it bred, but the pay was generous, and my boss was wonderfully lax. "They let me go six months ago. Apparently, editors and letter writers are no longer needed. We've all been replaced by software. I'm living off the severance—barely."

Roni cocks her head in sympathy. "That sucks. Are you still on Derby?" When Roni and I met, I was living in the back half of a yellow house, a nice little space I should have hung onto.

"God no—that place was way too small for Becca. We moved into an apartment on Ellsworth. The rent isn't bad, but I need to find something cheaper." My history, I realize, sounds mawkish, as if in

13 years all I've managed to do is lose things. I am 43—what will I sound like at 80? That's what aging is, I think now: just one long string of subtractions. But I don't feel like a loser, not yet anyway, and I sure don't want Roni to look at me that way. As I try to think of explanatory footnotes, high points to balance out the low ones, Roni says:

"I like it that you still color your hair."

Well yes, that's one thing that hasn't changed. When I was in my twenties, I got tired of my dull brown shag and decided to go platinum and short—very short. As if finally unleashed, this bold, spikey look took charge; I haven't been able to get out from under it since. Each time I consider something different, my hair says, *Oh no you don't.*

"I'm getting tired of it," I confess.

She rests her chin in her palm, smiles at me. "You look great," she says. "The same." Roni is a person, a subspecies maybe, for whom honesty is a reflex. The compliment makes me blush, and I am more grateful for it than she can know.

The bar is filling up now, couples and small groups streaming in, eager to leave the world behind them. Bowls of popcorn have appeared on the tables; the music is louder and faster; two bartenders are shaking and pouring. Happy Hour has arrived—a little late for me and Roni. We've had our drinks and shared our stories, and this unbound hour does not pertain to us. Ready to leave, I am not ready to say goodbye.

"Where are you staying?" I ask.

"Leslie put me up—she still has that house on Cedar." Leslie is an anthropology professor at the University. She has a large house broken into three apartments; Roni used to live in one of them.

"She had a free apartment?" I ask, surprised.

"No. I'm using her couch—it folds out." For a moment I am hurt that Roni didn't ask me, and then I remember: she didn't know I live alone.

Trying to sound casual, I ask Roni what her plans are for the evening, and she shrugs. "Not much. Sleep. I'm leaving at 5:00 am tomorrow. It's an eight-hour drive to Bend."

What can I offer to give us more time? We've just had dinner, so that's out, and I sure don't need another drink. I didn't eat enough to absorb the wine I've had; between that and the buzzing energy around us, I feel reckless, as if I can handle any bad decision I might make.

Where's the harm, that's what I'm thinking. Roni comes back to my apartment, stays the night, leaves at dawn. Whatever happens, or doesn't, where's the harm? What do we have left to lose?

So I throw out a wild card. "You want to meet Phil?"

She looks at me quizzically. "Who's Phil?"

"My dog. He's a mutt. Beagle and dachshund and something else."

"A rescue dog?"

"Of course. We can take him for a walk, maybe cruise the old hood."

Roni considers this a moment, then shakes her head. "I really should get going. I need to use Leslie's computer to send some paperwork up to Bend." I have a computer, too, I almost say.

"Oh—I've got something. Just for you." She unzips her backpack and reaches inside. I'm thinking she has an old photo of us, maybe a memento of some place we've been. What she pulls out are flyers, advertisements for Wild Ways. "You can start with a weekend course. They're easiest, but you still learn a lot."

I take the brochures and thank her, pretend to be interested. They are covered with pictures—women posed on snowy hills and river banks, arms hooked together, triumphant smiles. Roni doesn't want to sleep with me. She wants to save my life.

A few minutes later we are outside Vitus, hugging goodbye. "I'll be in Bend for three months," Roni says. She steps back, leaves her hands on my shoulders. "Promise me you'll think about taking a course." I promise her I will.

I won't. I'm not a wild woman and never will be. Knowing this helps, makes saying goodbye a little easier.

A Walk in the Park

Erin propped herself up and regarded her foot, which was twisted inward and starting to throb. "Goddamnit," she said. "God*damn*it." She looked back down the path and called out to her husband, who appeared a few seconds later.

"What?" he said, rushing over to her. "Are you okay?" He was puffing from exertion.

She pointed to her foot. "I stepped in that damn hole." She hiked up her pant leg, and Keith squatted down for a closer look. He placed his hand on her ankle, whistled softly.

"Wow. You really did it, didn't you? How bad does it hurt?"

"Bad."

Keith pulled his cell phone out of his pocket. "No signal." He considered, frowned. "I hate to leave you here, but I need to get help." Erin's eyes widened.

"I know," he said, "but we don't have a choice—you'll have to be carried out." He took off his jacket—Erin had left hers in the car—and settled it over her shoulders, then handed her a bottle of water and the bag of trail mix. "I'll be back as soon as I can. You'll be fine. Don't worry." He kissed the top of her head and hurried away, his red T-shirt flashing through the trees.

Slowly, testing, she moved her foot. Streaks of pain shot up her ankle and made her cry out. The hole she'd stepped into was nearly a foot wide and several inches deep. Freshly dug. This was no animal burrow, not right next to the path, nor did it look like a sinkhole. Who had done this? Some hateful child? She eyed the trees, her heart speeding up. A psychopath. The kind you heard about on the six o'clock news. Dark-eyed stalkers with matted hair. Quiet towns.

Unspeakable crimes.

Erin forced a deep breath. She needed to stop these thoughts.

Thank god Keith had come with her—she had almost left the house without him. They should do something fun, she'd said, something different. It was a beautiful fall morning; they needed to get out and enjoy themselves. How about a drive into the parklands? Standing behind him, she rubbed his shoulders and regarded the deep lines in the back of his neck, the widening patch of pink scalp, and he looked up from the newspaper he was reading and said fine, whatever she wanted to do was fine. His bland expression, his indifference to the options in his world, irked her. It was not like they had a surfeit of these days to spend together.

"Is there something *you* would like to do?" she pressed, to which he lifted a shoulder and turned back to his paper. "Not really."

"Never mind," she said, turning her back on him and walking out of the room.

"Wait," he called out. "Just give me a second."

"I'll be out front," Erin said, knowing how long it would take her husband to get ready—Keith never did anything quickly. She spent several minutes pulling small weeds from the flower bed, and then she stood up and studied the two burgundy plum trees flanking the driveway. For years they had mirrored each other; now, inexplicably, one was lush, the other spare. A pleasure turned into an annoyance. Beyond taking both trees out and starting over, what could she do? She should have planted shrubs—trees got away from you, took off on their own.

Keith came out of the house carrying their windbreakers, two bottles of water and the Garmin. He had also traded his loafers for a pair of Adidas. "Do you want to drive?" he asked, opening the door of the Range Rover. Erin slipped into the passenger side. "Not especially. Do you mind?"

He shook his head and connected the Garmin. "There's some trail mix in my jacket. And here's this," he added, reaching into his shirt pocket and handing her some folded squares of toilet tissue.

"Just in case." Erin was always kidding Keith about his Boy Scout ways, which, she had to admit, had saved her many times.

"Thank you," she said. "All systems go?"

He paused, his hands on the wheel, and looked down at her feet. "You're wearing those? What if we do some hiking?"

Erin buckled her seat belt. "Just drive, please."

*

Erin shifted position. How long before Keith returned? Were there rescuers available at a moment's notice? There had to be. She could not be the first person to injure herself in Kings Canyon.

And just minutes—*minutes*—before she fell, she'd been ready to call it quits, to admit, at least to herself, that Keith had been right about the cheap pair of slip-ons she was wearing. She was tired, too, ready for the comfy sanctuary of the Range Rover and a hotdog at Taylor Brothers—a meal she'd been thinking about for the last hour. Now they'd be heading to the hospital. There would be the wait in the ER, after which she'd be wheeled into to an exam room, where she would sit half-dressed on a cold table and wait for a doctor, who would then send her to some other part of hospital where she would wait for X-rays. God knows when they'd get home.

Something raced across her fingers. She jerked her hand and saw a large black ant hurrying away. Now she saw another, and another. She let her vision go slightly out of focus so that she could see only movement, and sure enough they were everywhere—she could be sitting on their nest. The thought made her jump, and fresh bolts of pain ricocheted around her ankle. "Ow!" she yelped.

Impossible that she should be stranded here, lodged among bugs and sticks and pine needles. She was sitting at her kitchen table just a few hours ago, playing Words With Friends on her iPhone. There was her toaster, her coffeemaker, her bright blue KitchenAid mixer. There was Keith pouring a cup of French roast, the hair on his balding head sticking out on one side.

She spied another ant heading her way. He paused at her fingertip, then skirted around it and resumed his urgent mission. Ants were always busy, always going somewhere. This was their world, not hers. She was just a big clumsy human, an obstacle to work around. The thought calmed her, made her think of Gulliver's Travels. These were not fire ants, she reminded herself, they couldn't hurt her.

But what about other bugs? What about spiders? Her mailman had gone camping in a park and wound up losing a chunk of his thigh. The doctor said it was a brown recluse. They lived in debris, she'd read, in rotting logs and outhouses and rock piles. She eyed a ragged tree stump a few yards away, then saw, just inches from her left leg, a small hole in the ground. What lived in a hole like that—snakes? Were they found in these altitudes?

She looked up then, at the dark pine trunks and the great grey rocks beyond them, at the pieces of rushing water she could see through the trees. There was a ledge on the upper left side of the picture, and her mind colored in a mountain lion ready to spring. It could happen: There were cougars in these parks, black bears too—she had seen pictures of them on a sign near the entrance. Keith had paused at the sign to read the warnings. "You're not supposed to run from a bear," he told her. "You're supposed to play dead."

What about mountain lions? She didn't think you were supposed to play dead with them. To a bear you were a nuisance, to a mountain lion you were fair game. The thought made her face and neck turn warm. Could cougars smell sweat? Is that how they tracked you?

A man in Orange County was killed by a mountain lion few years back. He had stopped to fix his bike, and the animal sprang out of the bushes. That same day a woman cyclist was attacked—hauled right off her bike, presumably by the same beast. It clamped its jaws around her head and started to drag her away, but her companion grabbed onto the woman by her ankles and kept pulling back until the cougar let go. Now *that's* a friend. Erin had no idea if she possessed that kind of courage; she wouldn't bet on it. She had once saved an exhausted Dachshund from drowning, but no heroics were involved.

The trouble she had caused! Insisting on taking a side trail, not the main one, the one Keith recommended, and then not keeping pace with him, forging ahead willy-nilly, taking her eyes off the trail to admire the bounding river. Now look at her. She couldn't even stand up, let alone run for her life. She felt awful—not just about this, about everything. She was a selfish, foolish woman.

She started to cry then, almost like an experiment, testing her capacity for despair. She cried quietly, then loud enough to hear her own sobs, and after a few moments she stopped. Any fool could do better than this. For the first time in her life, she thought how strange it was to cry. Crying was not a solution; it was the opposite of a solution, a pass you gave yourself to feel as wretched and useless as you possibly could.

*

Odd that on a day like today no other hikers had appeared on this path. She checked her watch. Considering how long it had taken them to reach this point, Keith would be gone at least another hour.

The pain in her ankle had turned dull and insistent. She bent forward, pulled up her pant leg, and slowly, grimacing, rolled down her sock. The news was not good. A mauve bruise had already wrapped around her ankle, which was ridiculously swollen, and her foot was not pointing the way it should. She tried bending it back to a proper position, but the sharp pain made her nauseous. If she had not broken her ankle, she must have done something equally bad, maybe worse; torn ligaments could take longer to heal, she had heard, than bones.

Erin lifted the bottle of water—the extra one Keith had been wise enough to purchase at the entrance—and took a long drink. She was thirsty in a sudden, savage way, and now that the shadows were longer she was grateful for the jacket Keith had thought to bring along. What a prudent man she had married.

Decent, too. Almost to a fault. Eight years into their marriage he had come into the kitchen, tears in his eyes, to confess an affair. It hadn't lasted long, just a few months, but it was over now; he had ended it. He was so sorry, he said, several times, and yes she could see that he was.

Erin was not irreparably wounded by this news; mostly she was irritated: Why had he felt compelled to report a problem he'd already fixed? Now she was shackled with it, forced to imagine her husband's stealth, the number of lies she'd believed. Having weathered her own indiscretion (a tax attorney named Jack), Erin was familiar with the subterfuge required. It was an awful way to live, split down the middle, no place to rest. Because this tormented chapter was over and done with, because she loved her husband and wanted to stay with him, she could see no value in lobbing back her own shameful story, and so she hadn't, and she wouldn't. Adultery was a dark business; the fewer dragged in, the better.

*

Staring at the patches of sunlight on her jeans, Erin startled at the sudden arrival of a blue jay, darker and prettier than the jays in Visalia, with a perfect pointed crest. It gave her the eye a couple times and hopped around her legs, unconcerned with her presence—that's how long she'd been stuck here; if this were nest-building time, the bird would probably be going for her blonde ponytail—well, it was mostly gray now, but she still considered herself a blonde, refused to change this fact on her driver's license.

She breathed in deeply: sun-drenched pine needles, warm boulders, cold clear water. Paradise, ordinarily. She used to long for this kind of solitude.

Something moved then, a brown streak across the rocks. Erin tensed, peered between the tree trunks. All she could hear was the river.

She tried to think what it might have been, some sort of rodent maybe, or a snake soaking up the sun. Maybe just her eyes playing tricks on her.

She did feel a little woozy—no surprise; she'd had nothing to eat today but a slice of rye toast with her coffee. Her stomach felt hollowed out, forgotten. Grilled pork loin—that's what she'd planned for dinner, with roasted red potatoes and green beans. She saw the pork now, rubbed with dry sage, waiting on a plate in the fridge.

Bonnie, her daughter, would be wondering why she hadn't phoned; they chatted on Sunday afternoons. Bonnie lived in Oregon, along with her forest ranger husband and his two children. Erin didn't think much of David, or the life he'd handed her daughter: a no-frills cabin eighteen miles from nowhere. All Bonnie seemed to do was drive those kids around, while contending with fallen trees, poison oak and ticks. It broke Erin's heart to remember the way her daughter once was, all that hope and silliness. Bonnie didn't laugh much anymore, at least not on the phone, and she looked older than she should. She claimed she wasn't unhappy, though, and last Christmas, when she and David had come to Visalia for Christmas, Erin had seen how much her daughter adored him. That's what love did, swept away the practicalities and left nothing but its own urgency. She'd sure gone crazy over Jack. She still thought of him now and then, in a tender, distant way, bewildered that all that ardor had simply vanished: a small fierce storm, like a dust devil in an open field, here and gone.

And just then, just as clearly as she had seen the pork loin in the fridge, she saw the shoebox in the back of her closet: a trove of cards and notes from Jack, photos too. The box she meant to throw away but hadn't.

Beau, her Golden Retriever, had posed a similar problem. His ashes were still in a wooden box on her dresser, thirteen years now. The plan had been to scatter them under the pepper tree in the backyard, where he used to doze, but so far Erin had not been able to do this, was not ready, would probably never be ready, to be left with nothing at all.

But Jack's letters, those could have consequences; she'd been careless not to destroy them. Alarm shot through her chest.

Not one person had come down this trail. What if she'd been walking by herself, which she did from time to time, and had to spend a night here? At this altitude, this time of the year, it would be like sitting in a meat locker all night. Hypothermia, that would be her real problem, not black bears or cougars.

Erin thought about this, what might happen, what Keith would uncover, if she never came home again, if here, or in a car, or at the mall—massacres happened all the time now—she perished.

Their joint savings—he'd come across that soon enough. Two years ago her sister Rose had started up a spicy pickle business. The pickles were excellent—everyone said so—and all Rose needed was $15,000 to help get her started. Keith, who owned a profitable hardware store in town, said no: Rose had no business plan and no real marketing strategies, and throwing good money after bad would not help her, and while Erin had agreed with his logic, she could not refuse her sister, not Rose, with her big heart and bad stutter. And so she had taken the money from the account, and given it to Rose, and lost it like Keith had known she would, and for the past 18 months, she'd been trying to put it back. To supplement her regular paychecks from the drugstore, she started writing—erotica, as it turned out. Alice, one of the other cashiers at Visalia Drug, told Erin that she paid for her daughter's orthodontia by writing stories for a British magazine called Knickers, and that they were always looking for new authors, and you used a pen name so what was the harm. Writing erotica, Erin discovered, was not difficult, requiring more nerve than imagination. She wrote about a dozen stories, and was paid quite well for them, before losing interest in the topic of titillation and the wanton characters she was spending too much time with. Because of this, the savings account was still depleted, and Keith would wonder why (he wasn't typically involved with the household bookkeeping, trusting her with these matters). At some point he would come across the cancelled check and learn what a liar his wife had been. The cards from Jack would undo him, and God knew what he'd think of the erotic stories lurking in her computer—something else she had failed to eliminate. This litter would be her legacy.

Erin didn't know how long she'd been snarled in these thoughts before she slowly turned—she wasn't sure why—and saw the weasel. She gasped, flinched hard. The animal didn't move. It stood on slim haunches, maybe five yards away, an inquisitive thing, about a foot and a half tall, with short rounded ears—lit pink by the sun—bright dark eyes and a golden underbelly. The face and sides were cinnamon-colored; the feet were clawed and sinewy. The small paws, resting lightly on the weasel's chest, gave the animal a look of patience, even kindness. Erin doubted this was true; more likely the little beast was sizing her up, waiting for a chance to move in. Her immobility was probably confusing to a creature that moved like a ribbon in the wind. This must be what she had seen on the rocks.

"Hello," Erin said, demonstrating her calm and supremacy. The weasel's paws twitched, and it leaned slightly to one side as if trying it get a better view.

"What? You've never seen a person with a sprained ankle?"

The creature kept appraising her. She looked straight back at its glistening eyes, its tiny muzzle and delicate whiskers, and she smiled. "You *are* cute."

She had seen photos of weasels but knew nothing about them. For all she knew, this one was gauging her vulnerability, planning its return after dark when she wouldn't be able to defend herself. But looking at its still features, its diffident posture, she did not feel threatened. She felt—there was no other word for it—pitied. Who knew? Wolves mourned, dogs were loyal; who could say a weasel didn't possess charity?

Still, it was odd to see one this fearless, and in broad daylight, and so in case it was rabid, or crazed in some other wild way, Erin was relieved when the animal lowered its slim body to the ground and, with a last glance over its shoulder, disappeared into the forest.

*

A chill breeze lifted the cuff of Erin's shirt and blew across her cheek. She looked again at the hole, where all her troubles began. Her punishment, it seemed now.

If a person had not dug the hole, what had? What else could move this rocky earth? A bear. It had to have been a bear. The animal had probably smelled something, an ancient Clif bar maybe, and started digging. Erin considered the bag of trail mix on her lap. She and Keith had had a couple handfuls on the way, but there was still quite a bit left. Maybe she should get rid of it, fling the bag as far as she could. Or should she eat it now, quickly? But that would make her smell like nuts and chocolate, wouldn't it? Erin eyed the woods again. She knew so little out here.

No. She would not think about bears or mountain lions or freezing. She would think of useful things, of steps she could take to set things right. She would think of her house and what she needed to do, and undo, once she got back there. Any moment now she would see her husband's red shirt coming up the path; from there she'd be fine.

Fire and Rescue

"So how many bodies have they found?"

"About 1100," Kelly said. "But there are probably hundreds more in the parts of the city they haven't excavated, thousands in the surrounding countryside. People who were on the road when the surges hit."

Donald removed his glasses and began wiping them with a small blue cloth. "What do you mean, *surges?*"

"Pyroclastic surges. Huge walls of ash and gases and molten rock. Super hot and super fast. Nothing would have survived them." She sliced the last of the cucumber into rounds and slid the pieces into a large bowl. "The surges hit Pompeii the day after the volcano erupted."

Donald put his glasses back on and frowned. "I don't get it, the lag time."

Kelly put down her knife and looked at his lanky frame sprawled on her sofa. His balding head shone under the ceiling light.

"It happened in stages. First there was the explosion, around noon, then this huge mushroom cloud that shot up 20 miles into the sky. That's when the pumice started falling. It fell for hours. Buried Herculaneum and Pompeii." She picked up the knife and reached for the radishes.

"Anyway, the pumice started to let up around dawn the next day and that's when lots of people who hadn't escaped earlier tried to leave. They thought the worst was over—it wasn't. What happened was, the mushroom cloud finally collapsed and sent these surges down the mountain, six of them. The fourth one reached Pompeii."

"That's awful," Donald murmured. "I wonder if there were any clues that the volcano was going to erupt."

"Oh there were clues. Lots of small quakes for weeks, even months, beforehand. Problem was, tremors were common in that area. A few people probably got nervous and left, but most of them didn't." Kelly tossed the green radish tops into the trash and pulled some salad tongs out of a drawer. "They thought that everything was run by gods back then. Maybe they figured that if they prayed hard enough, sacrificed enough innocents, the gods would save them."

She held up two bottles. "Ranch or blue cheese?"

*

Kelly herself did not believe in deities—one or many, just or unjust. Clearly, a god who sprinkled the world with both butterflies and botulism could not be credited with reason. Prayers or no prayers, we were on our own. This was a world of staggering wonder and we knew just enough about it to forge a blind path through.

If she were careful, Kelly figured, very careful, her money would last four more months. She'd already dumped her Cobra health insurance, her cell phone, her chiropractor, her hair dresser and Netflix; food costs she'd adjusted with lower expectations. Rent, utilities and car payments were non-negotiable.

How quickly it had happened! There she was, elbow deep in whole wheat flour, and then she wasn't. The day she was hired at the Big Dog Bakery, the owner of the shop, a well-dressed woman named Bonnie Pride, had said, "We get busy here. How are you under pressure?" Kelly had assured her that pressure was no problem, that after 20 years of line cooking and private catering, there wasn't a kitchen in the world she couldn't tame. And indeed that was the case. Rolling out peanut butter biscuits and carob cat cookies for Piedmont's pampered pooches was nothing compared to the hellish muck of restaurant cooking. And how much more gratifying it was to feed dogs! Their thumping tails and eager tongues, their ardent whimpers and unbridled worship. Kelly took to the Big

Dog Bakery like a spaniel to a duck pond. She loved the wholesome smell of it; the bins of tiny training biscuits; the toys and rainbow leashes; the photos and watercolors: golden retrievers running on beaches, blue tick hounds leaping over fences. Inspired by the fun, Kelly created daring new treats, outrageous mimics of human food: cheesy éclairs, applesauce cupcakes, oatmeal donuts, mini garlic pizzas. As the menu grew, so did the clientele, and Bonnie, who understood money and was generous by nature, rewarded Kelly handsomely. Sixteen months after Kelly was hired, Bonnie cut the ribbon on a second Big Dog Bakery in San Francisco and plans were made for a third shop in Carmel.

It was stunning what people spent on their dogs; you could be offended if you wanted to. Kelly thought her customers were wonderful: each day she was reminded that in this savage world there were people intent on bringing simple joy to animals—more people in fact than you could imagine. The Piedmont and San Francisco stores both flourished, with sales well in excess of target profit margins.

Who could envision an end to it? Who could have guessed that, one soy milk bone at a time, sales would taper off? People who shopped at the Big Dog Bakery were immune, or so Kelly had thought; the idea that they were tightening their purse strings, that they *had to*, made her woozy. As the weeks grew leaner Bonnie was obliged to shelve the blueprints for the Carmel site, and then to close the San Francisco store. At last she bid a teary farewell to most of the staff in Piedmont, keeping only Kelly and Deirdre, the girl who made deliveries. For a time Bonnie worked the register and even helped out in the kitchen, learning from Kelly how to make the bestsellers, which is all at that point they were bothering with. Bonnie wasn't a natural baker, neither organized nor quick, but by then it didn't matter. A few months later she closed the shop. Losing sight of the bakery, Bonnie and each other, Kelly and Deirdre floated away.

*

170

Kelly tried to picture the scene, to understand as best she could. The volcano spewed pumice all afternoon and through the night. Fires flared on the mountain and lightning flashed above it. The sea pulled away from the shore, stranding creatures large and small on the ash-covered sand. Boats in the harbor slammed into pieces. Earthquakes heaved the streets, cracked the buildings. Under the weight of volcanic debris roofs began to collapse.

People stumbled in the dark on the mounds of pumice, blankets tied to their heads. No one knew where to go. Those in houses ran into the streets; those in the streets took cover in buildings; people in boats rowed madly for shore; people on the shore sprang into boats.

Many, searching for loved ones, cried out to them. Some railed at the gods, others begged for mercy. They all must have thought that the world was ending, that hell had broken loose.

*

"Things are going to get a lot worse before they get really bad," Trish said. "Did you hear about that Tent City near Sacramento? Now they're laying off the goddamn garbage collectors."

"What?" said Kelly. "What's going to happen to all the trash?"

"Apparently we're not making enough. Especially businesses—they're not filling their dumpsters."

Of course, Kelly thought, struck anew by a casualty she hadn't considered. Of course the dumpsters would be empty.

"And people aren't getting their teeth cleaned. That's what Emily said yesterday—she's my hygienist. I told her to cheer up, that all this neglect means a big payoff later. I told her that when this mess is over they'll be up to their molars in money."

Kelly laughed. "What did she say?"

"She said that by then lots of people would need oral surgery instead of fillings. Emily is very serious about teeth. Hey, what are you doing next week?"

"Not much."

"We're going to Belize. Carl has to meet with some macho. Do you want to house-sit?" Trish and Carl had a home in Piedmont complete with tennis courts and a Roman-style pool.

"Sure," said Kelly.

"Great! Figure out what you need—we'll leave a check on the bar."

"Trish," Kelly sighed, "I should be paying *you* to stay there."

"That's not true. You'll be feeding the dogs."

"I love your dogs."

"So water a couple houseplants if it makes you feel any better."

Trish used to shop at the Big Dog Bakery. She came in every week and bought a variety of treats for her two greyhounds, Lily and Cleo, who sometimes accompanied her. Unlike other dogs that had to be restrained or scolded, Lily and Cleo always entered the store gingerly, like well-behaved children, looking all around, eyeing Trish for guidance. Both were rescue dogs who had spent their first three years muzzled, shunted in and out of cages, on and off race tracks. Perhaps their gratitude ran so deep they could not recover from it. It was a feature of greyhounds, she had learned, this abiding courtesy.

Trish was one of their few customers who shopped till the bitter end. Money was not an issue for Trish, nor was it likely to become one. Carl, her husband, brokered military food and sold to countries all over the world; as long as there were wars, coups, guerillas and gangs, Carl would do fine. Unable to help herself, Kelly once asked Trish how he could justify his livelihood. Trish shrugged. "With Carl it's strictly business—find the food, find the buyer. But you know, he does gobs of charity." Certainly Trish made plenty of donations. On the counter at the bakery there used to be a box for ASPCA contributions. While most folks tucked quarters, ones or fives in the slot, Trish offered checks, one of which Kelly caught a glimpse of: $5000.

*

Some of the victims were found clutching keys to houses they would never return to. Many had taken jewelry—silver necklaces, gold rings; some had seized their spoons and goblets; others fled with figurines, gods or goddesses they hoped might help them. A few carried modest amounts of money.

Eighteen bodies, some with their arms around each other, were found in a small room in the gladiators' barracks where they must have taken cover on their way out of the city.

One unlucky slave still wore his iron leg bands. Donkeys, tethered to mangers, were trapped inside a bakery. Tied to a post, curled in agony, was a forgotten guard dog.

Hunched inside houses were the sick and the old—those who were free to run but couldn't.

In the homes, in the streets, on the roads out of town, nearly everyone perished. Only the very canny and swift would have made it out in time.

*

Driving over to Donald's place, Kelly wondered if she could manage without a car. The east bay bus system was pretty good; she could get to Donald's with one transfer. Jobs might be a problem though, especially on the weekends. Or if she had to work nights, god forbid.

Donald lived in the remodeled garage of a house in the Oakland hills owned by two gay men. Having lost his job early on, Donald had become proficient at finding ways to save money, a few of which he imparted to Kelly each time they saw one another. Insider knowledge, was what Kelly called it, stock tips for the poor.

Today he advised her to shop for groceries when she was in a hurry and to stick to a list. "Buy oats," he added. "They're cheap, they're filling and they're good for you."

Donald knew a lot about food—what was good for you and

what wasn't. Having worked in a health food store, he could advise an herb or supplement for whatever ailment threatened, and he talked easily and at length about cytokine production, macrophage activity and CoQ-10. Kelly wasn't sure that working at Renew had been a good career move for Donald. He had taken a job there after leaving Kinko's, where he'd been worried about the smell of ink and how it was affecting his liver. Before that he had worked at the Gap, where he became convinced that the lighting was harming his eyesight. He was thrilled of course to have found a job in a health food store, but Kelly thought it might have fanned the fire. With all those potions at hand it was just too easy for someone like Donald to imagine a need for them. Now that he'd been cut off—no more employee discount; no more Renew, in fact—he felt unprepared for the harm that might befall him.

Kelly looked at the struggling young bird in Donald's hands. He was chirping, a tiny constant tweet.

"Ferd looks bigger."

"He's gained two ounces," said Donald proudly. Ferd was a pigeon that Donald had found flapping on the sidewalk. Like most baby birds, he was ugly—bald and gray-skinned. Donald was trying to feed him pellets of brown mush but the bird, wobbling on the newspaper, kept dodging his fingers. "He'll find it in a minute. It takes him a while."

"Does he always chirp like that?"

"Only during the day."

"What are you going to do when he grows up? Are you going to keep him or give him back to his kin?"

"I don't know," said Donald. "I don't want to think about it. I hate the thought of him eating fast food his whole life—dropped French fries, dirty pieces of donut."

Donald adored Ferd. "We're birds of a feather," he had told Kelly. "Homely and alone." Donald made frequent swipes at his looks, lamenting them good-naturedly. He said that being a homely gay man was "just plain wrong." Kelly didn't consider Donald unattractive; he had a long nose and a long face, but she thought it made him look Victorian. She saw him in a cloak and top hat, using an elegant walking stick.

Kelly's eyes swept the cozy room: the maroon velvet quilt she liked so much; the scarred armoire Donald had bought for a song; the altar he had made—a redwood shelf on which he had placed crystals, a votive candle and a small statue of St Francis; the tidy kitchen nook with its glass jars of bulk grains. How many times had they sat at this yellow Formica table and chatted away the morning?

"It's nice and warm in here," she said. "I'm keeping my place at 59."

"Well, I'm keeping it warmer for Ferd—I don't pay utilities here." Donald had a sweet deal. Dale and Richard probably didn't even need the nominal rent they charged him. Dale owned a swank antique store in Berkeley and Richard worked in San Francisco. Kelly wasn't sure what he did, but it must have been lucrative, judging from the clothes they wore, the cars they drove and the three houses they owned.

"Trish thinks we shouldn't have bailed out Wall Street," said Kelly. "What do you think?"

Donald gently lifted Ferd, who was still cheeping, and put him back in his cardboard box. "I don't know anything about high finance. I only know low finance."

"She says we should have castrated them instead."

"Ouch."

"I guess she and Carl have lost a lot of money—not, you know, that it matters."

Folding up the newspaper, Donald shook his head. "I don't know what you see in that woman."

"Donald, she's not the enemy because she has money."

"I know, but look who she's married to. All those donations she makes? That's blood money."

Kelly shrugged. "Yeah. Well. Someone's got to give—god knows the government isn't. Did you hear our idiot governor wants to tax veterinary services?"

Donald stood up and walked into the kitchen. "Tea?" he asked, holding up a tin. Kelly shook her head. "Let's talk about something else. Tell me more about Pompeii."

Kelly leaned back in her chair and reflected. After a moment she said, "Well, they had this creed, this slogan they lived by: 'Eat, drink and be merry for tomorrow you die'—ironic, huh? They decorated their drinking goblets with little skeletons to remind themselves."

"Clever," Donald said, nodding.

"And they were pretty bawdy. They had plenty of bars and brothels, lots of graffiti and risqué art—little satyrs with big erections, that sort of thing. Phalluses were all the rage. They carved them everywhere: on the houses and shops, on the fountains, on the stones in the streets."

"*Really?*" said Donald, smiling from the stove.

"Yeah. They were supposed to symbolize power and fertility, good fortune. Almost like lucky charms."

Donald turned off the tea kettle. "That's how I've always thought of mine."

"Let's see," Kelly murmured. "There was no end of bloody entertainment in the Amphitheatre. Talk about extreme sports—but I won't go into that. Oh yes, the baths. They all went to the baths every day. Big social thing."

"I miss the baths in San Francisco."

"I thought you said you never went to the baths."

"That's why I miss them," he sighed.

"Well you might not have liked these. People actually used them for bathing. And remember, no chlorine back then. If you went in with a cut you were likely to walk out with gangrene."

"Ugh," Donald shuddered. "What about the food? Did they eat good?"

"Better than most of us," Kelly said. "Bread, fish, olive oil, cheese, fruit. Bad teeth though—no toothbrushes." She paused, trying to remember more of what she'd read. "The streets were dirty too. People tossed their trash out their windows. There wasn't any trash pickup, no one scooping up the donkey doo. In fact, one of the things they had the slaves do was clean the guests' feet before they came inside."

Donald brought his tea to the table and sat down. "Well, that was pretty civilized. So lots of slaves back then?"

"Half the population. They did all sorts of things. They lived with their owners."

Donald shrugged. "We have slaves too, only we call them personal assistants and we pay them cash instead of room and board."

"True enough."

"When you think about it," he said, "we have all kinds of slaves. Office assistants, janitors, dishwashers, fruit pickers, yardmen." He sat up straighter. "I'm going to be a slave myself."

Kelly cocked her head, waited.

"Dale and Richard are letting me clean their house. Fifteen bucks an hour. Not bad, eh?" His eyes widened then and he clapped his long thin hands on the table. "Oh! Speaking of yardmen, you have to meet their new gardener. She's Norwegian or something. Tall, blonde and butch—everything you like. Drives a big red truck." He grinned. "*And* she wears a tool belt."

Kelly rolled her eyes. "Romance is the last thing on my mind right now. And what if I did meet someone I liked? At some point I'd probably have to take my clothes off and I don't think I can do that anymore."

*

If she got this job, Kelly thought, she could take public transportation. She could walk three blocks to BART or she could take the bus. And unlike the education specialist position at the Oakland zoo, this was a job she was qualified for: creating upscale salads and picnic fare. No line cooking, no late night catering, just simple kitchen work she could do in her sleep.

Kelly changed lanes, glanced to her left at the rooftops of West Oakland. She never drove the Nimitz Freeway without thinking about the day it collapsed, killing six of the seven nurses who were in a van on the upper deck. The sole survivor was a friend of hers.

Pompeii was struck by a large quake too, 16 years before Vesuvius erupted. The city was still being rebuilt on the day it was destroyed for good.

She recalled the conversation she'd had with Donald, what he said about modern day slavery. He was right. There were countless things that people would rather not do for themselves, things that could easily be shifted to others. At least the Romans took care of their slaves, kept them fed and sheltered even after they'd outlived their usefulness.

How she wanted to go back in time—to see the ancients in their houses, to hear them speak! For all the research that had been done, so little was known. Between bombings, earthquakes, clumsy excavating, shoddy renovations, periodic looting and the heedless relocation of objects, countless clues had been lost. How were meals prepared? Where did the children sleep? How did the merchants maneuver their donkey carts on those narrow, rutted streets? Were there really so many brothels, or were some of those masonry beds simply places for the poor to rest?

About one thing we knew too much: the horrific way they died. There was something evil about those plaster casts, Kelly thought, those man-made ghosts. We should never have laid eyes on them, should never have seen the grimaces, the eyebrows, the belt buckles. Not skeletons, not mummies, they were not corpses at all. They were the living dead, prized from their hidden pockets in the earth, crouched between this world and the next.

*

Kelly folded the newspaper and set it on the glass coffee table.

She looked over at Lily and Cleo, curled up on their beds.

"Forty-seven thousand foreclosures." she said, "Eighty thousand layoffs last month—and that's just California." The dogs looked up, regarded her gravely. "And that job at Harvest? I didn't get it." Lily, concerned, rose from her bed and walked over to the sofa.

It had been a hideous experience. For one thing, Kelly had no idea that they were interviewing five other applicants that day. They were sitting on stools outside the office when she arrived. Kelly perched herself on the last stool and cast a sideward glance at the woman next to her, a blonde wearing a close-fitting red jacket, a short black skirt and black high heels. She glanced at Kelly with a mixture of disdain and pity, then looked away. Kelly scanned the others: two Hispanic men, one Hispanic woman and one other white woman in a stylish blue suit. None of them looked over the age of 30.

The first question she was asked was why she left the catering business to make "dog food." Kelly did not tell the truth: that she felt she had more in common with the family pets than the owners; that trying to make seared salmon for 12 on a flat-top stove without adequate venting was a challenge she'd grown weary of; that days starting at 4:00 am boning chicken thighs and ending at 2:00 am in a van filled with dirty dishes were days she didn't miss.

Throughout the interview Kelly smiled and listened politely, evincing as much false cheer as she could stomach, agreeing to every disagreeable condition. *Sure* she could lift 50 pounds. *Absolutely* she could work any shift. Her biggest plus, her resume, the interviewer scarcely glanced at, preferring to pose a series of inane questions. Why did she want to work at Harvest? In what ways did she see herself contributing to "the Harvest vision?"

"Do you want a treat?" Kelly asked. Cleo immediately got to her feet and approached the sofa. Both dogs wagged their thin tails uncertainly.

"C'mon, girls." Kelly led them into the kitchen, which looked more like a large study than a room where food was prepared. The refrigerator was hiding behind a slab of mahogany; the stove burners were covered with a glossy black panel; the oven she had never found. Kelly slid open a deep drawer and pulled out a jar filled with organic dog biscuits. Lily lifted an exquisite paw.

"Bet you miss my cheesy éclairs, don't you?" She unscrewed the lid, pulled out four biscuits and offered the first one to Lily whose narrow muzzle opened gently. Cleo, her lustrous eyes fixed on the next treat, waited her turn.

When the dogs had finished their biscuits and retreated to their beds, Kelly went to the pool room, her favorite place in Trish's house. It was a long, high-ceilinged room dimly lit with sconces. The walls were deep gold, stenciled with ivy and filled with figures from antiquity, perfectly rendered, the paints cracked and faded: a woman in a red toga reading to a child; a naked athlete throwing a discus; a man selling loaves of bread; a young girl with a stylus pressed to her lips; a series of flying cupids, their bows drawn. But the most impressive feature was the long rectangular pool of emerald water, in the very middle of which was a mosaic of three leaping dolphins. Donald, who had been here once, said it was the most pretentious thing he'd ever seen. Kelly nodded agreement. "Do you like it?" she asked. "I love it," he said.

Driving back to her apartment, Kelly noticed all the For Sale signs that had appeared just in the last week. They looked like warnings. You couldn't forget; you couldn't ignore the fact that people were leaving in droves, or trying to. Some were fleeing in the dark, deserting the homes they could no longer afford, turning entire developments into wastelands pocked with weeds and stagnant swimming pools. In Detroit there were homes selling for a dollar.

*

A stray cat appeared on Kelly's porch. It was a yellow tabby, underfed, under-loved, determined to be rescued.

Much as she liked cats, Kelly had never considered keeping one here, a block from Telegraph Avenue, in a house cut up into four apartments, hers on the upper story. She could not let it roam at will, not with the cars, the kids, the occasional loose dog; nor could she bear keeping it inside, dooming it to a litter box and a window. The cat was not concerned with these things; he wanted only a place to rest and something to eat.

After the first couple days the cat began to eat normally, not in that gulping way that made his shoulders lurch. It was clear enough he wasn't going anywhere so when the first bag of food was gone Kelly bought an economy size sack of Friskies with a coupon Donald had given her. The litter box she kept in the bathroom under the sink, an arrangement that seemed fine with the cat, who used it discreetly. Occasionally, seeing him staring out the bedroom window, Kelly would raise the lower pane—there was a broken branch in the oak tree onto which he could easily jump—but he just sniffed the air and declined. With all the hazards out there, who could blame him? There were plenty of people content with armchair travel—why not a few cats?

*

"Dale and Richard are splitting up," Donald said. "They're selling this house and the one in the city."

"Wow," said Kelly. "I thought they were the perfect couple."

"Me too. In all the time I've lived here I've never heard them fight. They don't even raise their voices."

"So who told you?"

"Dale, of course. Richard hardly talks at all. Dale came down this morning and told me that things have been stressful for a long time. He said they want to simplify their lives—I think they might be in over their heads."

"If they're selling two of their houses, I'd say you're right," said Kelly, twining the phone cord around her finger.

"He said the antique business is really slow, that people don't want to play fair anymore. He called it 'a yard sale mentality.' And I guess things aren't much better where Richard works."

"I know he works in the city but what does he do?"

"He works for a securities firm—he's a financial analyst. Anyway, they're laying people off and I guess his job is on the line, too." Donald paused. "So basically I'm screwed. No way am I going to find rent this cheap. Or free Wi-Fi."

"Don't worry," said Kelly. "At the rate houses are selling, you've got plenty of time." She looked over at the cat, asleep in his wine box under the window. "Come over for dinner, meet my cat. I'll make spaghetti or something."

*

In one of Pompeii's larger homes the remains of three people were found, two adults and a child, equipped with a pick and hoe. Some believe that they lived in the house and were trying to find a way out as the pumice rose higher and higher. Others imagine that this was a party of looters who were killed when their tunnel collapsed.

In the weeks and months after the eruption, many tunnels were dug into the city. Robbers and treasure hunters—maybe a few surviving residents—risked their lives to take what they could: bronze, lead and marble; tools and trinkets, anything of value. By the time they were excavated, some of the grandest homes were found nearly empty, their walls scarred with holes.

*

Grating a chunk of cheese, Kelly wondered if she and Donald could live together here. It would be close quarters—one of them would have to sleep in the living room—but it would save them a lot of money. The armoire might not fit. And what about the pigeon and the cat?

182

She remembered a story then, a show she'd seen on TV about pet rescue. It was after a big flood and a van was going through the ruined neighborhoods picking up the animals that had survived. When the van stopped, a drenched dog or cat would scramble in and lay right down; they actually made room for each other. They forgot they were natural enemies.

She and Donald, the bird and the cat, maybe the four of them could figure it out.

*

When Donald arrived Kelly opened the wine and told him all about her interview at Harvest, the five other applicants, the questions she was asked.

"What a bitch! She really said 'dog food?'"

"Yes. You should have seen her. Self-important twit. And she was a child, they all were." She paused. "It used to be so easy, Donald, getting a job—I'd just walk in and start cooking. Not anymore. Now I'm 53. I'm invisible."

"You don't look your age," Donald said.

"Do you think I should color my hair?"

He shrugged. "Why not?"

"I don't know," she said. "It feels like I'm betraying myself. It feels….morally dangerous."

Donald rolled his eyes. "You are so dramatic. People have been marketing themselves since they started walking upright. There's no shame in it. You wear mascara sometimes, I know you do. It's the same thing."

"It's not the same thing. Mascara washes right off. If I color my hair now I'll have to do it forever."

"Not forever. Just till you get a job." He smiled. "Get a job, then let yourself go."

The cat, having finished a snack in the kitchen, stopped to sniff Donald's pant leg before crossing the room and leaping into his box.

"Have you named him?"

"Of course. I call him Julius, for his golden color and the nicks in his ears. But I think his days of battle are over. He's resting on his laurels now. How's Ferd?"

"Good. He's a little bigger, starting to look like a pigeon."

"You're a good father," said Kelly. "Making that bird baby food every day."

"Thank you." He took a sip of wine, looked around the room. "What's this music? I like it."

"It's a CD Trish gave me. 'Dinner in Tuscany.' Accordion music—who knew?" Kelly leaned back in the chair, propped her feet on the coffee table. "You know what I read in the paper? People are trashing their own homes. Well, not *their* homes, the banks' homes—people who've been foreclosed on. Anyway, they're so angry at the banks that they're yanking the appliances out before they leave, even the countertops, and selling them. Some of them are marking up the walls and ripping up carpet just for the hell of it, just so the banks have a harder time selling the houses."

"That's awful." Donald shook his head. "We're awful, aren't we? Vandalism. Greed. Waste. War. And now look what's happened." He turned to her. "It's like Pompeii, isn't it? Do you think the gods have abandoned us?"

"No. I don't think they were ever watching us."

"Well that's pretty bleak," Donald said.

"Is it more comforting to think that we're being punished? That the people of Pompeii deserved what they got? Look at all those temples they built, all that worshipping. Where did it get them?"

"Maybe they were as corrupt as we are. It sounds like it, from what you've told me."

"I'm sure they were. People are flawed, they always have been. We're flawed and we're vulnerable."

He blinked. "So that's that? Faith is pointless? No one is looking out for us?"

Kelly lifted the bottle, poured them more wine. "Donald, I'm making Spaghetti alla Carbonara. It's going to be good. Julius has a bed. Ferd is gaining weight. What do you want from the gods?"

Odds and Ends

On the last morning of her life Connie Zimmermann opened her mailbox and pulled out a fistful of ads. An oil change and rotation special at Big O, a timeshare offer from the Disney Vacation Club, a fried chicken special at the Bonfire Grill, an URGENT notice from Greenpeace, and a pork chop and rib sale at Schmick's Market.

What sad things mailboxes had become, Connie thought, as she made her way back to the house. They used to hold intrigue, the sort of mail you waited for: handwritten letters you read sitting down, news that made you smile, news that buckled your knees. Now your mail had nothing to do with you. Now you could be anybody.

Not that her mailbox was entirely useless. A few weeks earlier Connie had opened a notice from Prudential and wound up ordering long-term care insurance for both she and Wayne. Seventy percent of the population, the letter stated, would need extended care. And it was something you had to jump on early, while you could still afford the premiums—while insurers were still *offering* them: many companies, spooked by rising costs, were dropping out. Not so long ago, she would have tossed the letter in the trash, but this was the sort of information that kept her awake now. She was 57, Wayne was 60; it was time to pay attention, time to stop assuming they were exempt from ill winds. There had been no point in discussing the matter with Wayne, god love him—she was the one in charge of their safety. Connie did not hold this against her husband, did not even regard it as a shortcoming. She and Wayne flowed down separate channels, filling the common pond of their marriage. Wayne's dreamy ways had been vexing at times but never a real problem. So far.

Was it her imagination or was Wayne becoming more distracted? Much of what she said to him lately he either forgot or never heard. She did not of course expect him to absorb everything—they'd been side by side for 37 years—but sometimes when he slipped away, left their shared life for another, Connie grew frightened. She did not know where he went, and even though he was back soon enough, in a blink or two, she could not help thinking about his mother's demise. Ida had suffered from Alzheimer's for too many years before it killed her, and Connie did not think she was strong enough to lose her husband that way. Fortunately Wayne's father died just before Ida got really bad, before she started screaming obscenities at the dinner table and making passes at her own son. There was probably nothing wrong with Wayne, but Connie felt better having those insurance policies in place.

The walkway from the house to the mailbox was pointlessly long, and Connie could feel the sun burning her scalp. Great fluffy clouds were building in the west, thunderheads in the making. Weather was seldom a surprise in Kearney; you could see it coming from all directions, giving you time to run for cover. Homes, not looking for any trouble, were low to the ground and close together. Yards were unadorned, with lawns that tended to peter out before reaching the street. Trees were tough and oddly shaped—the weather turned them feral.

Still, Connie liked living here, not so much for what the town offered as for what it didn't: traffic, crime, crowds. She and Wayne had moved to Kearney from Omaha six years before, when an etcher at the Worley Monument Company died, leaving the job open. After nearly three decades at J.F. Bloom, where he had learned his craft, Wayne was ready for a change and Worley was happy to hire him. Wayne was one of the best, everybody said so. It wasn't just his craftsmanship, it was the way he worked with people, steered them toward just the right words and pictures. There was nothing stuffy about headstones anymore. If your hubby loved gambling, you could have his memorial etched with dice and cards; you could even arrange for an image of his grinning face. Wayne believed in headstones, understood that people needed them more than they anticipated. The world could be spinning apart, splitting open, but these markers, made of granite or bronze or Georgia marble, stayed in place, held their value. One time when she and Wayne were walking through Forest Lawn in Omaha, studying the headstones he had etched—elaborate, funny, heartbreaking—they stopped before a child's memorial: Kaylin Eve Courange, June 2007 to July 2008. Wayne had etched the baby's handprints on the left, her footprints on the right. Hushed, Connie cast her gaze over the legion of headstones rising from the grass, each one waiting for a passerby, each one whispering the same two words: Remember Me.

Connie shut the door against the heat and headed down the hall to the kitchen. She had washed the breakfast dishes, wiped the counters and swept the floor, leaving this room as tidy as the others. Messy homes confounded her; she could not fathom people who gave up their only stronghold. Dropping the mail into the trash can under the sink, she paused a couple seconds over the Bonfire Grill special. The photo was fetching: three pieces of golden chicken next to fluffy mound of mashed potatoes and a biscuit dripping with butter. No. She had lost 13 pounds by not eating this kind of food, and she had another 17 pounds to go. She did not want to wind up with diabetes, which is where she was headed, according to her doctor. For the past couple months she'd been preparing low-fat meals and eschewing dessert, a regimen that benefitted Wayne as well—lean as he was, his cholesterol was high. Now and then Connie would come across bakery receipts in her husband's Subaru, but she kept quiet, believing that marriage was an alliance, not a stranglehold, and you had to allow for a few glazed donuts.

On the kitchen table were the items she was taking with her: a stack of old towels for the animal shelter, a pair of eyeglasses in need of a new nose pad, and a list of items Wayne wanted from Ace Hardware. Connie took one more satisfied look around her kitchen, admiring the crisp yellow curtains and cheerful orange countertops, then lifted the receiver from the wall phone and dialed Bernie.

"Hello?"

"Good morning," said Connie. "It's me. You about ready to head out?"

"Sure," Bernie. "Sooner the better. I'm watching the news, that movie theater shooting. Horrible."

"Yes, it was," said Connie, who had heard more than enough about the maniac in Colorado—news that bad was hard to avoid. Wayne still read the Kearney Hub each morning, while Connie did not, depending on her husband to apprise her of any pertinent local events. She had once been able to accommodate the news, however disturbing, but age seemed to be thinning her nerves, along with her hair and skin. Danger was imminent, she knew this, could take on no more trouble.

"I have a couple stops before Ace—is that okay?"

"Sure!" said Bernie, who had to be the most obliging person Connie knew, a quality that made it easy to do her favors: Bernie didn't drive. This had not been a problem when Bernie's husband was alive, and as far as Connie was concerned, it was not a problem now. Bernie did have two children, daughters, but they both lived out of state, and one of them, Stephanie, was useless anyway, only visiting when she needed money. Hard to believe that such a shiftless, black-hearted girl came from a mother like Bernie, but that was parenthood: You had no idea what you were unleashing. Connie and Wayne had been fortunate, winding up with David; quietly and in private, they still remarked on it. They had wanted another child, but Connie miscarried. Perhaps the baby was unwell, or would be; in any case they did not try again. They had used up their luck, or so it seemed.

Doug, Bernie's husband, had died the previous winter, just two months after he was diagnosed. He started having dizzy spells, which Bernie thought had something to do with his ears or his bad sinuses. What he had was brain cancer, the sort that spreads like ink and for which there is no vocabulary. It did not matter what questions Bernie asked the doctors: the answer was no.

The four of them—Wayne and Connie, Doug and Bernie—had been close. They used to eat dinner together on Friday evenings, alternating houses and menus, playing cards or Yahtzee afterwards. Doug's death was a collective blow absorbed individually. For several weeks after his funeral, Bernie skirted any mention of her husband, avoiding him like a closed door, but as the weeks went on, she began to make allowances. "Doug would have *loved* that," she would say of a new recipe, or, "Doug always said the mayor was a fool." Not long after that she would cite his shortcomings, rolling her eyes in mock exasperation: "That man drove me crazy—had to switch on every light in the house." Grief turned some people into dry wells, but Bernie, who found little in life to argue with, made her peace with death as well and so reclaimed her husband. Connie admired Bernie and had often pondered her irrepressible cheer, deciding it was not a quality you could adopt but one you were favored with, like keen vision or a strong heart.

Bernie lived just four houses down from Wayne and Connie and was waiting at her mailbox when Connie pulled up. As always, she greeted Connie with a big smile, then slid neatly into the car, nimble for a woman her size and age. With her steadfast pageboy hairstyle and stout figure, Bernie reminded Connie of a Campbell Soup Kid, and indeed she looked younger than her 65 years, which was one advantage of carrying extra weight—it smoothed out the wrinkles. Connie thought her own face looked older since she'd started the new diet, though Wayne said that was nonsense.

"I love that outfit," said Connie. She and Bernie had gone to Sears the week before and Bernie was wearing the items she bought: white shorts and a yellow top that exposed a generous portion of her slack freckled breasts. That she was no longer young and firm did not seem to concern Bernie, as if age were a law she chose to ignore.

"Thank you," Bernie said. "You look nice too. That's a good color on you," she added, pointing to Connie's blouse.

Who didn't look better in pink, Connie thought, which is why she had three pink blouses and a pink dress, even a pink bathrobe: pink was a serviceable color. While Connie liked to look her best, she gave little consideration to her attire and seldom bought new garments. There was a time when clothes shopping was a thrill, when a new dress could make her giddy, but those feelings had subsided, and any purchases she made now were only to replace something frayed or stained, bringing her the same satisfaction she might get from new shelf liner. Which was fine. Connie didn't mind being past the age when clothes were lures and each day was burdened with high expectation.

"It's a hot one," said Bernie, buckling up. "Looks like we're going to get some storms."

"I think you're right." Connie eyed the treetops, which had begun to sway as if in warning; the solid trunks looked ready, defiant.

Driving down the wide open streets of Kearney still gave her pleasure. Aside from the friends she and Wayne had left behind and that perfect kitchen with its big pantry, there was little she missed about living in Omaha. Both she and Wayne had grown up in Broken Bow, and Connie was glad of that, thankful to have been raised in a cozy community where people looked out for each other, but she was ready to leave when Wayne started working at the monument company. People in Broken Bow knew everything there was to know about her, or thought they did, and Connie wanted to be someone else: someone daring, or kinder, or smarter, someone at least mysterious. And then there was the massive feedlot just south of town where thousands of cows were fattened for slaughter. As a child, happily immune to worlds outside her own, Connie had not considered the cattle, had not even minded the odor that soaked the town on hot summer days. It wasn't until she was out of high school that images of those animals, their bright panicked eyes, began to take root in her, to become a chronic affliction. She stopped eating beef, hoping that a clear conscience would save her, but her tiny pledge made no difference. The cows were still there, and all she could do was leave them behind. Opportunity for Wayne, escape for

Connie, Omaha rescued them both; 30 years later Kearney did the same.

"Where to first?" Bernie asked.

"The animal shelter. I'm dropping off some old towels."

"What a good idea," said Bernie, slapping her thighs. "I should do that. I have a couple blankets I don't need."

Connie looked over. "Do you want me to turn back?"

"Oh no. It's going to take me a while to find them." This was true. The closets in Bernie's house were overflowing with the paraphernalia she used to make Christmas decor: Styrofoam balls, squares of red velvet, sequins, rickrack, gold cords, miniature nativity scenes, tiny sleighs and mangers. Bernie fashioned these whimsical ornaments all year long and sold them to friends and local gifts shops, then put her earnings in an IRA. Clever gal, that Bernie. She'd worked in cash management at First National and was good with her money; it probably wasn't by chance that Doug had carried such a sizeable life insurance policy.

They were on Route 30 now, heading west. Just above the pale horizon, the clouds had massed into a huge gray slab from which sleeves of rain emptied onto fields and towns. A plastic bag whipped across the road and plastered itself against a church sign: "Today's To Do List…Thank God." Fast food cups skittered by, followed by a wheeling paper plate. To the left, a lone dog trotted down the middle of the sidewalk.

"Wonder where he's going," said Bernie. "I don't see the owner."

"We're almost at the shelter," said Connie. "Let's see if we can get him in the car." She put on her turn signal and pulled over, but when she opened the car door, the dog gave a worried look over its shoulder and broke into a sprint.

Connie shook her head and slid back behind the wheel. "Let's tell the folks at the shelter. Maybe they can send someone out."

"Oh I'm sure they can. Poor little guy."

Connie drove on. By the time they pulled into the shelter the sun was gone and the sky had turned a yellowish-gray. She should probably skip Lind's Optical, but her old glasses were giving her headaches, and the store wasn't far. "You coming in?" she asked, lifting the pile of towels from the back seat.

Bernie shook her head. "I'd better not. You know how that goes." And yes, Connie did. Bernie had adopted three cats from this shelter and was feeding a stray. Connie had brought home dogs, two on the same day, a black lab and a pit bull mix. Dick and Jane. They were adults at the time of adoption and so their ages could only be estimated, but Dick, the lab, was clearly older than Jane. His face had gone gray and he walked with effort. The dogs kept continual watch over each other, monitoring subtle changes of mood and responding with a lift of the head, a tentative tail wag. After Dick, there would be another dog, there would have to be, on account of Jane.

The girl behind the desk regarded Connie without interest, her thumbs poised over her cell phone. Connie described the dog, some sort of terrier, she thought, with light brown fur. "Can you send someone out? It can't be far—I just saw it."

The girl shrugged. "Maybe Louis. When he gets back from lunch."

"When will he be back?"

"I don't know," the girl sighed. "Not long. We only get a half hour." From the back rooms came the howl of a dog, a plaintive, pointless note. Other dogs, roused to hope, began to bark.

"I tried to get him in the car," Connie said, "but he was scared." She placed the bundle of towels on the counter. "Anyway, I know you can always use these."

The girl frowned at the towels. "Yeah, thanks. We have a lot of them already, but whatever." She turned back to her phone. Her round face was raging with pimples; even without them she would not be attractive. Connie understood her grudge against life, but this place was too fragile for rancor.

"You need to be nice," Connie said, "If you can't make the effort you should quit." The girl looked up, stunned, and Connie walked out. She would never have spoken up like that when she was younger, and she was pleased with herself. People said that age took away your inhibitions, but Connie thought it took away your blinders, made you see how many things depended on you.

"They'll send someone out to look for the dog," Connie told Bernie, getting back behind the wheel. "Supposedly."

"I hope so," said Bernie, frowning with concern. "How are Dick and Jane, by the way?"

"Fine. We've had to up Dick's Cosequin, but he's doing pretty well. That stuff is amazing—I don't think he'd be walking without it." Connie pulled onto the main road and got behind a vintage Oldsmobile traveling well below the speed limit. At each intersection the car slowed to a crawl, the driver apparently not trusting the traffic lights.

"For the love of Pete," Connie murmured, stepping on the brake again. "Of all days."

"Maybe they're having car trouble," Bernie offered.

Connie laughed. "I'd say so."

Finally the driver signaled a turn, and the Oldsmobile swung wide to the left. Connie could see the driver now, a tiny white-haired woman, and she felt bad for laughing. She pictured herself at 85: muddled, half deaf, peering through clouds of cataracts. And that's if she were lucky, not wheelchair-bound or worse.

The sky was darker now and more bits of trash whirled across the road. A sheet of newspaper, caught on a light post, shivered in the wind. Just as they drove past Dollar General, a large black O fell from the yellow sign and bounced down the sidewalk.

"Golly," Bernie murmured. "That could have hit somebody."

Connie accelerated, drove as fast as she dared: five miles over the speed limit. Seven miles was the cut-off, that's what Wayne had told her; the police didn't bother with anything under that.

Connie glanced over at Bernie. "I have to pop into Lind's Optical. You okay with that?"

"Sure, honey, whatever you need to do." Bernie glanced out

window, then turned back to Connie. "What do you hear from David these days?"

David was an anesthesiologist. He worked at Scripps Health and lived in San Diego, which is where he wanted his parents to move when Wayne retired. "The weather's perfect," he told them, "year round. No more shoveling snow, Dad. No more black ice." Naturally, Connie wanted to be near her son, but she wasn't at all sure about California with its earthquakes and high taxes and long naked coastline. She liked living in the middle of the country, no jagged edges, just wide open land farther than she could see, farther than she could imagine. And she had come from this land, was a measure of it. Maybe it was foolish to think this, but Connie wondered if, like plants, people did best in the place they were born in, if the air and soil of Nebraska were nourishments she would falter without. Maybe she was just afraid of change.

Their son, their only child, a doctor, an achievement she and Wayne had little to do with, having determined early on to be tolerant parents, to accept middling grades and modest athletic performances so that David would be spared the humiliation Wayne had suffered. Connie well remembered Wayne's father, Karl Zimmermann, his narrow eyes and near constant scowl, his coarse brown hair sticking straight up. Even when he got sick and Wayne was over there every day helping out, he could not find a tender word to say, just sat on his porch and glared at the world.

"We just spoke with him yesterday," Connie said, smiling. "He's good. He's fine. Oh, get this—he and Jamie are getting married." Jamie was a dermatologist; she and David had been living together for nearly three years, sharing a condo near the hospital.

"Oh my," said Bernie. "That's wonderful. Are they having a baby?"

"That's what I asked. No, they're not." They were almost at the mall. Connie switched on her signal and pulled into the left turn lane. "I don't think they're going to have kids—where would they find the time?"

Bernie nodded. "Two doctors. Isn't that something?"

When he was in residency in Omaha, Connie asked her son why he wanted to be an anesthesiologist, why that instead of, say, a cardiologist or a pediatrician, and he said he liked the idea of taking care of people, keeping them safe, while other doctors did their work. Not until David starting working at Scripps, holding his patients in that eerie, unassailable stasis—Connie saw it as a deep red labyrinth—did she began to apprehend the risk involved, the reason for his stratospheric insurance premiums. What a brave man her son was! Connie had undergone general anesthesia just once, when she had her varicose veins stripped. Excited at the prospect of normal-looking legs, she had not been apprehensive about the surgery. It was the consent form she had to sign the day before that gave her pause. Dying itself did not scare her—everyone died—but Connie wanted to be present for her death, to feel herself slipping from this world into the next. She wanted that grand surprise, saw it as part of the bargain.

There weren't many people at the mall, and Connie was able to get a parking space right in front of the optical store. "Be right back," she said.

Bernie smiled pleasantly. "Take your time. I'm going to text Brenda." Brenda was Bernie's other daughter, the good one, the one with four children and Bernie's pretty blue eyes.

Dominique, the woman who did the eyeglass repairs, came out of an office in the back. She was a wiry woman with short black hair and dark skin. Darker freckles of varying size spotted her nose and cheekbones. As always, she nodded and beamed at Connie, her wide white smile overtaking her face. When Connie first met Dominique she assumed the woman was uncommonly friendly, but when she smiled back and said it was nice meeting her, Dominique pointed a finger at her mouth and mouthed the words, *can't talk*. Laryngitis, Connie concluded, or a recent surgical procedure, but this was not the case. One of the sales gals let Connie know that Dominique was a mute, and Connie realized that the nodding and beaming was how she communicated. Having no voice, she presented a smile, a peace offering, the world's first language. Connie thought it was a sweet way to be, and she wanted to share these feelings with Dominique but did not know how.

The sky looked odd when Connie came out of the store, a charcoal mass from which hung lighter lobe-shaped clouds, rows and rows of them. They had a name, Connie was sure of this, but she couldn't remember what it was. She got back into the car and pointed up. "What are those called?"

Bernie peered through the windshield, grimaced. "Storm clouds."

"Ace and then home," said Connie. "Hopefully we'll miss the worst of it."

"They say we're going to have a snowy winter," Bernie remarked.

"Then I'm glad I'm buying a new snow shovel." That was on the list. Their old shovel had snapped in two and Wayne wanted to make sure they replaced it before winter. He also wanted weather-stripping and a back-up roll of duct tape. Bernie needed a sink stopper and another bird feeder.

"Well, at least you'll get a little break in November, you lucky so and so," said Bernie with a wink. "That was so thoughtful of David."

Connie's face softened at the sound of her son's name. "Yes it was."

As an anniversary present, David was sending Wayne and Connie to Maui, a gift that included their stay at the Hilton, along with a luau and a helicopter tour. Connie was looking forward to this, having read the brochures and scrolled through online pictures. Paradise, that's what everyone called it. Palm trees, pink sand beaches, wild orchids; the islanders spoke English, and you didn't have to worry about parasites or foreign currency. (David had actually given them a choice. Knowing that Wayne had a robust interest in his forbears, David had also offered them a trip to the Mosel Valley in Germany. Wayne said either option would be fine with him, so Connie, picturing gloomy castles, heavy foods and people she could not talk to, made the decision.)

A few minutes later Connie and Bernie pulled into the parking lot at Ace Hardware. This time there were no available spaces in front of the store, so they parked a short distance away. As they were walking past a green Volkswagen, Connie noticed a woman with long blonde hair in the passenger seat. Her hands were covering her face, her shoulders were heaving. Connie gaped, looked away. How awful it was to see a stranger crying. The woman's business was her own, but walking past her felt wrong, like leaving the scene of an accident.

"That woman was crying." Connie said.

Bernie looked around. "What woman?"

Connie tilted her head toward the car. "The one in the Volkswagen."

Bernie peered behind them, shook her head. "Poor soul. You never know, do you?"

"No," said Connie. "You don't." Sickness, maybe. Or a broken heart. Maybe something too awful to speak of.

"I know just where I'm going," Bernie said as they entered the store. "Meet you at the front." Familiar with the store's layout, it did not take the women long to locate what they needed, and in just a few minutes, they were back outside, bags in hand. In her other hand Connie held the new snow shovel like a scepter, its wide flat surface rising above her head.

"Darn," said Connie. "Too late." The rain had begun, fat drops exploding on the pavement, pelting their heads and faces. The air was dense, pungent with asphalt and ozone.

Connie looked at Bernie, at her faultless hair, her flimsy sandals. "You stay here. I'll get the car." Bernie started to protest, but Connie was already gone, hurrying across the parking lot, her shovel jerking wildly.

Bernie never saw the lightning; her phone chimed with a new text from Brenda just seconds before the ground stroke hit. She did hear the terrible crack of thunder, and then she saw Connie, sprawled in the lot.

Bernie would not remember dropping her bag, running to her friend, would not remember falling to her knees and taking Connie's hand in hers, would not remember the deepening puddle she was kneeling in. What she would remember was the rain pattering Connie's face, her calm expression, her knowing eyes, which blinked several times before they stayed open. For the rest of her days, Bernie would remember Connie's arm rising, her finger pointing to something Bernie couldn't see, and the last words she uttered: "There," Connie said, "*there.*"

People would blame it on the snow shovel, would claim that lightning struck the shovel and killed Connie Zimmermann in an instant. This would not be true. The mighty bolt that felled Connie ignored the tiny shovel and detonated on the earth itself, scorching the air and sending its jagged volts 60 feet in all directions. The currents that hit Connie traveled up one leg and down the other, knocking her flat and halting her heart. The snow shovel was thrown three yards; the hand that held it was not harmed—there had been no time for flesh to burn. The only marks on Connie's body were just below the skin, red rivers of burst blood vessels on her legs and torso that looked, strangely enough, like bolts of lightning.

The odds of being killed by lightning are three hundred thousand to one. Though Connie was unaware of this statistic, she would not have been surprised to learn that she was the one. Somebody had to be the one, and wasn't she somebody?

She could not have said what hit her, was not even sure that she'd been hit. There was only a blinding brightness, and then, slowly, a darkness that fell in velvet folds all around her, and she was somehow moving through this soft dark toward a small glowing screen. It was as if she were watching a movie from a distance, a beckoning scene both familiar and unknown, the colors more vivid as she grew closer. She was nearly there, could see the colors turning into shapes, her path unfurling between them. There it was, had always been, another world, a promise kept. More than anything she wanted to tell Bernie, to let her know about this lovely place, but she was inside it by then and on her own.

ACKNOWLEDGMENTS

These stories appeared, in slightly different form, in the following journals:

"Chasing Zero": *Four Ties Lit Review*, Vol 2 Issue 1, Summer 2012

"In the Company of Crows": *The Blue Lake Review*, May 2013

"Manatee Gardens": *The Blue Lake Review*, June 2014

"Nine Glorious Days": *Eunoia Review*, December 2013

"The Songbird Clinic": *Summerset Review*, Fall 2013

"Breach": *Crack the Spine*, Issue 54

"Parasites": *Summerset Review*, Spring 2015

"The Golden Age": *Halfway Down the Stairs*, September 2015

"Lovers and Loners": *Four Ties Lit Review*, Vol 1 Issue 4

"Fire and Rescue": *Eunoia Review*, July 2013

"Happy Hour": *Minerva Rising*, Issue 5

"A Walk in the Park": *Digital Papercut Literary Journal*, Vol 1 Issue 3

"Savages": *The Milo Review*, Vol 2 Issue 2, Summer 2014

"Odds and Ends": *Crack the Spine*, Issue 177

"Salvage": *damselfly press*, Issue 36

ABOUT THE AUTHOR

Jean Ryan's stories and essays have appeared in a variety of journals and anthologies. Nominated several times for a Pushcart Prize, her debut collection of short stories, *Survival Skills*, was published by Ashland Creek Press and short-listed for a Lambda Literary Award. Her novel, *Lost Sister*, has also been published.

In her recent book *Strange Company*, a delightful collection of short essays, Jean Ryan brings us closer to the natural world. From lizards to lady bugs, from the inscrutable sloth to the resplendent quetzal, Ryan reveals some of our commonalities with earth's creatures and hints at the lessons we might learn from them.

Praise for *Survival Skills*—

Publishers Weekly: "Ryan controls devastating psychological material with tight prose, quick scene changes, and a scientist's observant eye."

The Los Angeles Review: "With her debut collection Survival Skills, Jean Ryan brings to the short story what Mary Oliver does to poetry."

74027967R00115